HAUNTING AT HAWTHORNE HALL

PARANORMAL COZY MYSTERY

HAUNTED HISTORIES
BOOK TWO

LYNN M STOUT

CHAPTER 1

"Jackie? Earth to Jackie," Emily's voice was insistent. "Are you okay?"

"Yeah, I'm fine. I'm just thinking about Maplewood."

We were on our way to our next assignment, an old theater named Hawthorne Hall. As the van's tires hummed along the highway, I had became lost in thought.

"Do you know what ended up happening to Mia?" Emily asked.

"I don't know exactly about Mia," Ethan jumped in before I could respond. "But I checked in with the mansion a few weeks ago and they are up and running as a bed-and-breakfast again. The town bought the property, and it's going to be preserved as a historical landmark. I also connected with Clara again. She, uh, misses us."

I smiled. Clara was a local psychic, who led a seance for us and really, it was because of her we could solve the mystery. I was more than happy to keep up contact with her. And based on the smile on his face, it appeared Ethan felt the same.

"And they did eventually find Julia's skull in Mia's car. I told them to keep it far away from the mansion, just in case. I think it's ended up in a museum in town," I added.

"Was she in trouble for that, too?" Emily asked.

"No, although it took some explaining from me, but Mia wasn't in trouble for that. I mean, we all know she was awful, but no one wanted her to pay for something she didn't do. Speaking of which, she did steal from the company and they are pressing charges."

"Wow! It's not like ghost-hunting isn't enough. We have all this drama going on with the living, too!" Emily turned to Ethan and threw her arms around his neck. "I haven't said it enough, but thank you for bringing me with you. I love my job!"

The van pulled into a gravel covered parking lot and we were officially at our new filming and investigating location. Everyone peered through the windows as the van settled in front of the grand theater. Its once majestic facade was marred by years of neglect. Ivy clung to the walls, and the windows were clouded with grime. It gave the building an air of forgotten grandeur.

"Well, this is it, gang. Let's check it out." I climbed out of the van with Gabby, my African Grey parrot, perched on my shoulder as always.

"Hawthorne Hall, the theater with a thousand tales and, apparently, a few ghosts," Ollie, hopping out and stretching. She waited until her sound equipment was unloaded and swung it over her shoulder with practiced ease. I had to laugh at her chosen attire. She wore a Hawaiian shirt with cargo shorts and was rocking her red Crocs with socks.

"Let's hope the ghosts have something more exciting to show us than just their dust collection," Tyler added as his eyes scanned the building's exterior.

Emily was bouncing on her toes. "I can't wait to get inside and see what we find. The history of this place is incredible! Just wait till you hear everything Ethan and I discovered! We've been saving the best parts for when we arrived."

"Well, okay then. Let's get to it." I hesitated. "And stay safe, everyone," I added with a quick glance at Leo.

He smiled ruefully and rubbed the small cut that was sure to become a scar. I still hadn't fully gotten past the guilt I felt for what happened to him at Maplewood Mansion. And I needed to remember to give him the vitamin E oil I brought for him.

Our motley crew approached the grand entrance with enthusiasm and determination, as though going into war. Then we stopped. There were several doors leading into the theater.

"Which one?" Tyler asked.

"Not sure," I replied. We spilt up, each of us going to a different door until Ollie called out.

"This one!"

The heavy wooden door creaked ominously as she pushed it open. The lobby of Hawthorne Hall was just as grand as its exterior, with marble floors and a sweeping staircase that led to the upper levels. Dust motes danced in the beams of sunlight that filtered through the dirty windows, giving the place an ethereal glow.

"Okay, let's set up base here in the lobby," I suggested. "Ollie, you and Leo get started on the sound and video. Ethan, Emily, you're with me. We'll do a preliminary sweep of the theater while they set up the equipment. Tyler, will you be ready to record now or do you want to wait and explore with us?"

Tyler smoothed his hair and squinted into a small mirror he carried with him. "I'll wait. The drive gave me bags under my eyes."

As we spread out, Gabby flapped her wings

and settled on a nearby statue. "Lights, camera, action!" she squawked.

Gabby was going to have a blast in this place. It reminded me of the old movies and TV shows I watched with Grandma and I knew on some level she felt the same nostalgia.

As Ethan, Emily, Tyler and I moved deeper into the theater, our flashlights cut through the dim light. The main auditorium was vast, with rows of plush, red velvet seats and an ornate stage that spoke of a bygone era of grandeur. The silence was thick, broken only by the soft creaking of the building settling around us.

"This place must have been magnificent in its heyday," Ethan muttered, his flashlight beam sweeping across the rows of seats.

"It still has that feeling," Emily said in a hushed voice. "I mean, even with all the dust and everything, you can feel the history."

"I agree," I said. Ethan moved to the left and Emily to the right, while Tyler and I stayed on the stage. We kept a sort of respectful quiet as we crept around. The air felt chilly and there was a distinct draft. But to be fair, that wasn't unexpected in an old building like this one.

The hairs on my arms stood on end.

"Just a draft," I whispered to myself, as my flashlight revealed the intricate details of the theater.

Suddenly, Gabby's voice echoed from the lobby, loud and clear. "I see dead people!"

I turned quickly and saw Gabby flying through the lobby. I heard Ollie's voice loud and clear.

"It's okay, Gabby. Calm down, sweetie."

I knew Gabby was now sitting on Ollie's shoulder and she was being comforted. But I also knew it was likely she really saw something. I looked at Tyler.

"Just setting the mood?" He suggested.

Ethan appeared from the shadows, a wry smile on his face. "It does feel like we're not alone here."

"Yeah, I heard something too," Emily said, appearing from the other side of the stage.

"Okay then. Let's get back to the lobby. I want to check on Gabby."

Of course, she was fine. She was on Ollie's shoulder, supervising the process of setting up the soundboard. When Gabby saw me, she flew the few feet to land on my shoulder and nuzzled her head into my cheek. I ran my hand down her back. She seemed to have calmed down from whatever startled her.

Ollie turned to me and smiled.

"Find anything?" I asked.

She nodded slowly, taking off her headphones.

"We've got some strange interference. It's like static, but there's something else... whispers, maybe? Did you guys hear anything in there?"

"Sorta, but nothing clear. And it felt strange. You know that feeling...," Emily said.

Leo nodded. "All too well. I want to get cameras set up in there as soon as possible."

"Me, too. Let's go," Ollie said.

After they finished in the stage area, Leo and Ollie joined the rest of us back in the lobby. It was time for our team meeting where we would hear about the history of this place and then decide as a team what direction we would take for the investigation. But first, I had one piece of sensitive housekeeping to do. Just as I was about to tell everyone about our new producer, we all turned at the sound of high heels clicking across the lobby floor.

I groaned. I'd really wanted to give everyone a heads up before she arrived. Especially after our awful experience with Mia.

Instead, a young woman in her thirties clicked her way towards the group. She had a laptop bag slung over her shoulder. She wore an actual pantsuit and had her hair in a bun. Her heels were supernaturally high. How she could walk, I had no idea. Knowing Ollie was thinking the same thing, I stole a glance at her. I caught her looking at her own red Crocs and then at the woman's shoes. She smiled and looked at me, eyes wide and amused.

"Hello, everyone! Rachel Adams. I'm your new producer and I am so excited to be here!"

"Hello," Gabby said.

Rachel jumped, and then a loud belly laugh tumbled from her slight frame.

"Hello, to you!" She said. "What's your name?"

Gabby looked at me and turned her head to the side as though waiting for introductions.

"This is Gabby," I said, reaching out to shake Rachel's hand. "And I'm Jackie Thompson, the director." I went around the circle introducing everyone else, but it seemed I didn't need to. Rachel had done her homework.

"Yes, Tyler Reed. I love your voice-overs. Let's try to get a few more into this episode, okay? And Leo Kim, so sorry to hear what happened last time. I am determined that nothing like that will happen to my team ever again. We will keep all of you safe."

She turned her smile to Emily next. "Emily Nichols, I have heard good things about you! You have a wonderful career ahead of you. And your mentor, the famous Dr. Ethan Brooks. I've read everything you've written. Brilliant!"

Finally, she turned to Ollie. "The amazing Olivia Harris. You and Jackie make quite the team. Your reputations are spectacular."

Ollie raised one eyebrow and looked at me

helplessly as Rachel pumped her hand. "Uh, it's Ollie," she managed to say.

"Ollie, of course. And finally, the intrepid Jackie Thompson. Director extraordinaire and psychic leader." She stopped with an exaggerated sigh and collapsed into a vacant chair. She continued to smile as she looked around our small group.

I shook my head once and cleared my throat. How did she know I was psychic? I barely knew it myself.

"Rachel, we're so happy to have you here and to have you excited about what we're doing. Um, do you want to sit in on our first meeting? We're going over what we know and planning our investigation."

"Oh, yes, please," she said, scooting to the edge of her seat. "Don't let me keep you from anything. I'll just sit here quietly."

"Alright, everyone," I began, trying to project confidence. "Before we dive into the specifics of our investigation, I believe Ethan and Emily have some additional background on Hawthorne Hall."

Ethan cleared his throat and began. "Yes, we do. Most of you already know Hawthorne Hall was built in the late 1800s by Samuel Hawthorne, a wealthy industrialist who had a passion for the arts. The theater quickly became a cultural hub for the community, hosting many plays, operas, and concerts. It was a place where the elite of society would gather, and it thrived for decades."

Rachel nodded, jotting down notes as he spoke. "So, what changed? What happened?"

"Well, in the 1940s, tragedy struck. During a performance, a fire broke out backstage. Several people were injured, and two actors, Ned and Nellie Harper, were killed. The cause of the fire was officially determined to be faulty wiring, but there is a large number of people who believe there was sabotage."

"You mean someone started a fire on purpose? But why?" Rachel asked.

"That's part of why we're here," I said. "Keep going," I motioned to Ethan.

"The fire marked the beginning of Hawthorne Hall's decline. It struggled to regain its former glory and eventually closed its doors in the early 1970s. Since then, the theater has stood mostly empty, falling into the disrepair we see here."

"Mostly empty?" Leo asked, making air quotes around the word "mostly."

"There's a small troupe that has acting lessons here weekly and sometimes they perform for the community. Until recently, they would hold summer camps here and they've even tried to use the building for a yearly art festival, but as time goes on, it's become too dangerous and there are liabilities. The building is currently owned by the town's historical society. They are desperately trying to raise funds to renovate and keep it open before a developer buys it up."

"Huh, developers," Rachel huffed as she sat back in her seat.

Tyler looked at her and paused, with his mouth open as though he forgot what he was going to say. Then he seemed to remember and asked, "What about the hauntings here? What do we know about that?"

"This is the good part," Emily said. "Over the years, there have been many reports of paranormal activity. People have heard disembodied voices, seen shadowy figures, and felt cold spots throughout the theater. Some even claim to have seen the ghosts of Ned and Nellie Harper," she said. "If you're lucky, they will perform a show for you." The group smiled, and Emily sighed. "Can you imagine how cool that would be?"

Ethan continued. "The local historical society has documented many of these occurrences. They've been trying to preserve the theater and its history, but the hauntings have made it difficult to attract investors or support for restoration."

Rachel looked intrigued. "I have a note here that a Laura Bennett contacted us. She's the head of the historical society."

I glanced at my notes. "Yup. I have her name too. She's very involved in the preservation of

Hawthorne Hall and says if we can prove the hauntings are actually Ned and Nellie, and if we can get video or audio proof, she thinks that will help generate the support they need for restoration. She hopes our investigation will shed light on the theater's haunted history and bring attention to its plight."

"She thinks ghosts will help?" Leo asked. "Are we talking about ghosts like Julia from Meadowbrook Mansion?"

I couldn't blame him for asking. Julia was a force to be reckoned with, and after all the excitement from that adventure, I suspected everyone was hoping for a little less drama this time.

"No, not like Julia," I said. "In fact, the opposite. Laura provided us with a list of the most active areas in the theater. The main auditorium, backstage, and the dressing rooms are at the top of that list. There have also been reports of strange noises and sightings in the basement. And many have reported seeing and hearing Ned and Nellie around. They appear to be very friendly," I added.

Leo smiled and nodded, then adjusted his camera equipment, a nervous habit I'd noticed he developed. "Sounds like we've got our work cut out for us."

We all stood up and were ready to get started when Rachel interrupted.

"Yes, but first," she waved her hands at us. "We need to get to know each other," she said.

"What do you mean?" I asked. "We've already worked together so-,"

"Not you guys, silly," she said. "I need to get to know you. If we're going to work together."

I tried to tell her we didn't have time for games, but she was insistent. She explained she had college classes that prepared her for this role and one thing she always did was play a game called Two Truths and a Lie.

"It's one of the best ways to start a conversation and to get to know another person," she added.

Again, I tried to tell her we were short on time and that we already had been through quite an experience together, but there was no stopping her.

"It won't take long, I promise. I'll start. Okay. I own a horse. I was in a sorority. I stole a car. Now, guess which one is the lie!"

The silence was deafening, and it continued to drag on. I needed to move this along so we could get to work. Thankfully, it seemed Ollie agreed.

"Stole a car is the lie," she finally said.

"Yes! You guessed it!"

Ollie rolled her eyes.

"Okay, you're next."

Ollie took a deep breath and, in an effort to end the torture, threw out an easy one. "I robbed a bank. I like technology. I've known Jackie for decades."

Of course, we all knew what the lie was, but Rachel was insistent. "Someone make a guess."

Finally, Leo said, "Robbed a bank is the lie."

"Yup. You got it. Wow," Ollie deadpanned.

"Okay, Leo, your turn," Rachel said.

"I robbed a man a gunpoint. I was a drug dealer. I served time in jail for starting a fire in my high school."

"Oh!" Rachel said.

"Um, Leo, buddy," Tyler began. "I don't think you quite got the hang of the game. It's supposed to be two truths and one lie. Not three lies."

"No, I understand the game."

"So, two of those things are true?" Emily asked.

Leo nodded.

"Oh, my," Rachel said, covering her mouth with her hand.

I knew Leo fairly well and from interviewing him and doing basic background checks before hiring him, I was quite confident he did none of those things. Leo was very funny, but in a quiet way. He wasn't boisterous or loud, and he generally kept to himself. In fact, anyone who had worked with him before often expressed surprise at how open and talkative he was with us.

He continued to look around expectantly, waiting for us to guess the lie.

As the silence continued to drag on, I decided to put a stop to the game.

"I think I need to think about that one for a while. Let's finish the game later, okay?"

The team readily agreed, with happy nods and affirmations all around. Rachel, especially, seemed content to move forward with the investigation and leave the game behind.

With sighs of relief and more than a little confusion, we all stood and stretched. But before we could actually get to work, another set of shoes was clicking their way across the marble floors.

CHAPTER 2

A man was striding towards us, his expression stern and unwelcoming. He wore an expensive suit, and his presence exuded authority and disdain.

"Can I help you?" I asked, trying to keep my tone neutral.

"I'm Richard Hargrove," he announced, his voice cold and clipped. "I'm the developer who owns this property. What are you doing here?"

"We were invited by the local historical society to investigate the reported hauntings," I explained, meeting his gaze. "They believe our findings might help preserve the theater."

Hargrove's eyes narrowed. "Preserve it? This place is a relic. My company plans to tear it down and build a shopping plaza, or maybe a parking lot. Either is a better use of the space and will bring in more revenue."

Ollie stepped forward, her hands on her hips. "This theater is a piece of history. Once it's gone, it's gone forever."

Hargrove sneered. "History is fine, but progress is better. This town needs economic growth, not ghost stories."

Before the situation could escalate further, Rachel stepped in, her presence calm and authoritative. "Mr. Hargrove, we understand your position, but we're here to conduct our investigation. Our findings could provide valuable information that might change your perspective."

Hargrove glanced at Rachel, his expression softening slightly. "And you are?"

"Rachel Adams, the producer of this show," she replied, extending her hand. "We appreciate your concerns, but we have a job to do. If our investigation reveals significant historical or paranormal findings, it could affect your plans. We ask for your cooperation. And, according to my records, you don't actually own the property. The historical society does."

Hargrove hesitated for a moment, then nodded curtly. "Fine, for now. But don't expect me to support this endeavor. My company's plans are already in motion. And the sale will go through. Those hippies won't be able to stop me. I'll be sending my secretary over. She'll be the contact person for you. I don't expect to see or hear anything about this again." He waved his hand dismissively.

As he turned and walked away, I couldn't help but feel a sense of relief. Rachel had handled the situation perfectly, and her support was a welcome change from the confrontational attitude of our previous producer.

"Thanks, Rachel," I said, once Hargrove was out of earshot. "It's nice to have someone on our side for a change."

Rachel smiled. "We're all in this together. Now, let's get back to work."

Ethan, who had been quietly observing the exchange, suddenly spoke up. "Jackie, you might want to take a look at this." He was staring at his laptop screen.

I walked over and peered at the screen. Ethan had pulled up several recent articles about a local group protesting the demolition of Hawthorne Hall. The headlines read: "Save Our Theater! Community Rallies Against Development" and "Historical Society Fights to Preserve Hawthorne Hall."

"Looks like there's more going on here than we thought," Ethan said. "This group is pretty active. They've been organizing rallies and petitioning the town council to stop the demolition."

Emily nodded. "We should definitely talk to them. I'll reach out to Laura Bennett and set up some interviews."

~

I waited while Rachel made her call. Everyone else was too excited and ready to get started. After once again insisting everyone work in pairs, they spread out through the theater.

Ollie and Leo promised to stay together as they ventured deeper into the back rooms and into the basement, setting up equipment as they went. Ethan and Emily followed them, but their job was more nuanced. They were looking at the theater as historians and researchers. They wanted to find artifacts, written records, personal items, anything that might help the investigation, especially anything relating to Ned and Nellie.

Tyler was the only one who wasn't assigned a buddy. He was in the restroom in the lobby, trying to mask the puffiness under his eyes. It wasn't critical that he be on camera for the first part, but he wanted to be ready.

"Are you leaving him by himself?" Rachel asked as she tucked her cellphone away and made a note.

"Yes, he's only going to be in the restroom. I think he's safe."

Just as I said that, he stumbled over his own two feet and just barely caught himself before sprawling face first on the ground.

"Come with me." I said, taking her arm and turning her away. "Let's do our own exploring."

"Sure," she said. "And we can become buddies at the same time."

I wasn't sure how likely that would be, but at least she was better than Mia. "Right," I said. "Gabby?" I patted my shoulder and Gabby settled immediately. Rachel and I made our way into the theater section.

"Tell me about Gabby," she said as we explored.

I explained how she had belonged to my grandmother, but when she passed away, I inherited her. "Gabby is very smart," I added. "And she quotes old TV shows and movies. My grandmother would watch all the old detective and crime shows with her, so she picked up quite a vocabulary."

I didn't add anything about the times Gabby had spoken to me in full sentences and used words I didn't realize she knew. I still wasn't sure what was going on with that, but for the moment, I simply added it to the list of confusing and supposedly psychic things I was learning about myself.

"Let's check out the offices," I suggested to

Rachel. "Maybe there are some records still there, although I doubt it."

"Sure, you never know," Rachel said.

The building had power and the lights, such as they were, were on. But it was still dark and damp in the hallways behind the stage. Rachel and I used the flashlights on our phones to help navigate.

"We should have picked up our flashlights," I said as I pushed open an office door. "We're going to kill our phone batter- Oh! Crap!"

I yelled and jumped backwards, knocking into Rachel, who was standing right behind me. Gabby squawked and flew straight up, landing on the top of the door. As my heart beat its way out of my chest, and downy white feathers drifted around us, Rachel steadied me and peered over my shoulder.

"What the hell?" She exclaimed.

A well-dressed woman in her mid-thirties, holding a clipboard and exuding an air of professionalism, stood in the middle of the room. She turned with a mild smile and held out her hand.

"Hello, I'm Amanda Kerrigan. Mr. Hargrove sent me to assist you with anything you might need while you're here."

"So, you're not a ghost?" Rachel asked, still firmly planted behind me.

She laughed. "No. Not a ghost. A personal assistant. I've been tasked with ensuring that you have access to all areas of the theater and to provide any information you might need. If there's anything specific you're looking for, just let me know."

"What are you doing in here?" I finally managed to speak now that my heart was no longer lodged in my throat. "How did you get in?"

"Like I said. I have full access. I'm here to provide you with that same access. As far as why I'm here, well, this is the office, so I figured this is where I would settle in. If that's okay with you?"

"Uh, sure." I glanced up and motioned for Gabby to return to her perch on my shoulder. I stroked her back, making sure she was okay after our fright. I knew she was reacting more to my reaction than to Amanda's presence.

"Allow me to show you a few things," Amanda said. "Follow me." As she lead us from the office, she reached out and scratched Gabby's head. "Sweet bird," she muttered.

Despite how strange the interactions with her were, Amanda turned out to be very helpful. She knew of passageways through the theater that the actors would use when doing costume changes or when they needed to move from one part of the stage to the other quickly and unseen by the audience. She also showed us where a set of dressing rooms used to be before they were boarded up after the fire.

"The damage was extreme and well, this is where Ned and Nellie died. It was easier to board up the area and basically create a new wall. I don't think anyone has been in here in decades. Really, probably not since the actual fire," she explained.

I made a note of how to find the area again as we walked through the maze of hallways back to the manager's office. "Feel free to explore all these areas. I've left the doors unlocked for you. And do be careful in the boarded up area if you decide to go in there. It's been off-limits for so long, I'm sure there is rotting wood and who knows what else."

"Thanks, Amanda," Rachel said. "Your help will make our investigation a lot easier."

Amanda nodded and glanced at her watch. "If you need me, I'll be in the manager's office. Just call if you need anything."

With that, she walked away, leaving us to our investigation. As soon as she was out of sight, Gabby flapped her wings and squawked, "Nice lady!"

I scratched Gabby's head absentmindedly. "Yes, I suppose so."

Gabby was generally an excellent judge of character, but this time, I wondered if her instincts were just a tad off.

TYLER REED: TAKE 1

The camera opens with an aerial shot of Hawthorne Hall, a once-glorious theater now cloaked in the melancholy of neglect. The overgrown ivy clinging to its walls and the grime-covered windows hint at the secrets buried within. Tyler Reed steps into view, a practiced smile on his face, though his eyes reflect the gravity of what lies ahead.

"Welcome, everyone. I'm Tyler Reed, and tonight, we're delving into the shadows of Hawthorne Hall. Built in the late 1800s, this theater was once the heart of cultural life in this sleepy small town, a stage for the grandest of performances. But today, it stands as a haunting relic of a bygone era. However, echoes of the past may still linger in its darkened corridors."

The scene transitions to the grand, decaying

entrance of the theater, where the team cautiously enters.

"Tonight, we're not just here to explore the architecture of this forgotten gem, but to uncover the truth behind the tragedies that marred its history. From unexplained fires to mysterious deaths, the spirits of Hawthorne Hall may still be waiting in the wings, eager to share their stories. But are these just tales told to keep curious souls like ours at bay, or is there something more lurking in the shadows?"

The camera cuts to the team setting up their equipment, their faces lit by the eerie glow of their flashlights.

"Armed with state-of-the-art paranormal investigation tools and a deep respect for the past, our team is ready to venture where others fear to tread. Will we finally shed light on the mysteries that have kept this theater shrouded in darkness, or will Hawthorne Hall keep its secrets hidden forever?"

The scene ends with a close-up of the theater's stage, empty yet full of potential, as the camera slowly pans out to show the team's silhouettes, poised and ready for whatever comes next.

CHAPTER 3

L ater that day, we arrived at the town's community center, a modest building with a welcoming atmosphere. We were greeted by a diverse group of residents who sat in a circle of folding chairs. The room buzzed with their voices.

As we entered, a woman come up to us and introduced herself as Laura Bennett, the head of the historical society.

"Thank you for coming," she said. "I know you had expected just a few of us, but when word got out about what you're doing here, everyone wanted to pitch in and help. I think you'll get a lot of good background and some great stories from this group. We really do have a unique thing happening with the theater."

"Thank you for all of this," Rachel said as she

also shook hands with the older woman. "Where should we set up?"

Laura led Leo and Ollie away, making suggestions for camera angles and sound in the large room. Rachel followed them and within a few minutes, she gave me a thumbs up. We were ready to roll.

She stood at the front of the room and cleared her throat. "Thank you all for coming. I'll be quick and introduce Jackie Thompson and her team from the show *Haunted Histories*. As you know, they are investigating our very own Hawthorne Hall."

There was a round of applause, and a few people stood. As everyone settled back down, I awkwardly stood next to Laura. No one told me I'd be giving a speech today.

"Thank you, Laura. Uh, really, Tyler should be up here. He's the on camera person and knows how to do this stuff."

Everyone chuckled, and one person whistled.

"Um, anyway, we're honored to be here and to assist however we can. We already know some details about the theater's past, and we know your stories and insights will add so much more. We want to learn everything we can, so let's start with your stories. Then, with your permission, we might have a few of you speak one-on-one with Tyler on camera."

"Sounds great," Laura said. "Margaret, why don't you start?"

An elderly woman stood slowly and then sat back down. "I don't need to stand, do I?" She asked as everyone chuckled softly.

"No, of course not," Tyler said. Ever the gentleman, he scraped a chair across the cement floor while everyone cringed at the noise. Then he sat down next to her. "Please, go on."

"My name is Margaret. I've lived in this town all my life. I used to attend plays at Hawthorne Hall with my parents. It was a grand place, full of life and laughter. The velvet seats, the ornate chandeliers, the smell of fresh popcorn in the lobby... it was like stepping into a different world. Ned and Nellie Harper were the stars. They were like royalty around here."

"We understand there was a fire and Ned and Nellie were killed. Do you know if there were any rumors or suspicions about what caused it?" Tyler asked gently.

"Officially, they said it was faulty wiring. But there were always whispers. Some folks believed it was arson, that someone wanted the Harpers out of the way."

A young man spoke up. "Yeah, my grandma said the same thing. She believed it was no accident. There were too many strange things happening around that time. My name's Jake, by the way."

"Hi Jake," I said. "Strange things like what?"

"People heard voices when no one was there, saw shadows moving in empty rooms. Some said they felt a chill in the air, even in the middle of summer," Margaret said.

"Yeah, that stuff. And then on the night of the fire Gran said people swear they saw a figure in the rafters just before the flames erupted. But by the time anyone realized what was happening, it was too late."

"We would really like to do two things here," Ethan said. "We want to try to find out more about the fire, if it was deliberately set. And we want to investigate the current hauntings."

"Oh! The current hauntings aren't hauntings at all," Margaret clapped her hands. "It's Ned and Nellie doing their show!"

"Really?" Emily asked. "That's for real? They do a show?"

"Oh yes! I wouldn't say nightly, would you?" Margaret looked at Laura, who shook her head.

"No, not every night. But sometimes the activity picks up, and it's more frequent. Then other times we'll go weeks without hearing anything."

Emily laughed out loud. "Oh, my gosh! That's amazing! Who here has heard this show?"

Everyone in the room raised their hand.

Everyone started talking to each other telling their own version of the seeing the Ned and Nellie Show. As the room become more animated, I motioned to Ethan and Emily.

"Will you two try to talk to everyone here? Get as many personal stories as you can. Anything really interesting, take them to Tyler."

Emily began bouncing on her toes and clapped her hands. "Are you kidding? No way you could stop me! I want to hear them all!"

Ethan nodded. "Absolutely!"

I turned to Laura. "I would also like to hear more about the fire itself, especially if anyone knows of a possible motive or suspect."

"Ah, that would be dear Margaret," Laura said.

Margaret was deep in conversation with Tyler when we approached them. I needn't have worried. Tyler was already getting Margaret's take on the fire.

"Ned and Nellie were beloved by most, but not everyone," she was saying. "There were some in town who were jealous of their success. And there was talk of a rivalry with another theater group from a neighboring town," Margaret began in a mysterious voice.

"Please, go on," Tyler encouraged her.

"But nothing quite like what was happening

right there in the Hawthorne. There was a young man named Frederick Mason. He was an ambitious fellow, always looking to outshine the Harpers. Some say he would have done anything to see them fail. And what's interesting here, is that after the fire, no one has heard from or seen him since."

"Do you have any thoughts about that?" Tyler asked. "Do you think he disappeared because he'd done something?"

"Oh, sure. It's quite possible. And faulty wiring? Yet there's never been anything like that before or since? Please."

"Good point. That's very helpful," Tyler said. "A name we will look into for sure," he glanced at me, and I nodded as I wrote the name in my notebook. "Anything else you'd like to add?"

Margaret shook her head. "No, that's all. But Jackie, you won't find Frederick Mason anywhere."

"How do you know? I thought you said he disappeared."

"Well, he did. Into the theater."

CHAPTER 4

It was a quick drive back to the theater. We all were completely silent, which was very unusual, and I was a little worried.

But as soon as we busted through the doors of the lobby, we immediately sounded like the group at the meeting. Everyone talked at once and tried to raise their voice louder than the person next to them.

"Okay, okay!" I tried to get their attention. It wasn't working, they were too excited.

"Hey! Guys!" I tried again, to no avail.

Then Gabby let out a long, low and very loud whistle that had everyone stop in their tracks and look at her.

"Shhhhhh," Gabby added at the end of her whistle. Then she looked at me with her head tilted sideways.

"Sorry, Jackie," Ethan said. "Sorry, Gabby."

"Yeah, we got so much good stuff," Emily added.

"Right? Us too," Tyler agreed. "Sorry, Gabs."

"Okay, everyone, let's get back in our circle and share what we learned tonight. We can take turns and it'll be a team-building exercise around sharing information." Rachel was way too perky for this time of night.

Ollie glanced at me and rolled her eyes, but in a good-natured way and everyone took their seats.

"Well, I guess, Ethan, you and Emily start," I said.

"Well, long story short, every single person there has had a first-hand experience with some paranormal activity in the theater. They have heard laughter and applause. They've seen lights on when there is no power connected, and some have smelled burning wood," Ethan said.

"Right," Emily added. "And this woman, Anya, is a member of a local theater group who practices here. They have rehearsals and sometimes even do actual programs here. Anyway, she said she's seen Ned and Nellie first hand, said it was like she could have reached out and touched them. But she wasn't scared. She was very adamant that we understood that."

"Agreed," Ethan jumped back in. "Everyone was very clear that Ned and Nellie are completely harmless. Some went so far as to say they were a comforting presence."

"And Jake mentioned it's one of the reasons why they are fighting so hard for the theater. They feel special that they've been able to see Ned and Nellie and it's become sort of a mission to save them," Emily said. "He even said he's started acting because of them and their influence."

"Huh," Leo said.

"What Leo?"

"Oh, nothing. Just that's a lot of personal information, I guess."

I looked at Emily, who didn't seem to hear what Leo had said. She was engrossed in her notes. Then I looked at Ethan. His brow furrowed as he looked between Emily's bent head and Leo's irritated expression. He smiled slightly to himself.

I made a mental note to follow up on that later.

"It's good to get personal things like that, right Tyler? We want our interviews to be authentic."

"Absolutely," Tyler said. "And if you're ready, I think I got some genuinely concerning information."

"About the fire?" Rachel asked.

"Uh, um, yes." Tyler cleared his throat. "We heard about the darker side of this place. There are supposed to be hidden passages throughout the theater that the actors would use to move around quickly. One woman said her father was a caretaker here and discovered one of the passageways but, she said, he refused to enter it. Said it was evil."

"Evil?" Ollie asked. "So we have this loving amazing couple up here telling jokes and making people happy while an evil entity is creeping around below the stage. Sounds about right."

"Well, that may be a slight oversimplification of the situation," Tyler said. "But, yes, that about sums it up."

I looked at Rachel and nodded. "We had a little experience with those passages when we met Amanda. I would agree they are creepy, but I didn't feel evil. Rachel?"

She shook her head. "No, not that bad. At least not where we were."

I stood and stretched, then ran my hands through my hair. A habit I really needed to stop because every time I did it, the drier grey strands would end up sticking straight out. Ollie was kind enough to point that out to me not long ago. She informed me that I looked like a swamp witch who had just woken from a nap.

She gave me a little smile again and casually patted down her own hair. I took the hint and stuck the strays behind my ears as I began to pace.

Everyone stayed quiet, either making notes of their own, lost in thought, or simply letting me think. After a few minutes, I had two things, and I ticked them off with my fingers.

"First, I don't know about you guys, but I really want to see Ned and Nellie."

That was met with vigorous head nods and sounds of confirmation.

"Second, who wants to go looking for hidden passageways under the theater?"

That was met with a still silence.

"Okay, no worries, guys. It's late, and it's been a really long day. And honestly, I want to be the one who looks for the passageways. With my senses, I think I am the best option to find something."

Ollie caught my eye and grinned. I knew she was signaling how proud she was. And honestly, I was proud of myself as well. Still, learning to accept my psychic ability was proving to be a long process, but after the encouragement of the team and after how I found Julia's bones behind the mansion, I was feeling my own sort of encouragement.

"That's amazing, Jackie," Tyler said.

"Yes, wonderful to hear," Ethan added. "And I will join you, if you don't mind. It's not as foreboding of an idea if you are there, too."

"Thanks, both of you," I said. "We'll plan it for

tomorrow. For tonight, though, let's see if we can encourage Ned and Nellie to visit."

Everyone took it seriously. Emily made popcorn and Leo pulled out soft drinks from the cooler. We grabbed blankets and pillows and dragged them into the theater itself.

Leo and Ollie set up some additional recording equipment and double and tripled checked what was already there. Both crossed their fingers that it would pick up the performance and provide amazing proof for the show and for the group.

I crossed my fingers that there would even be a performance.

We sat in the plush seats and waited.

Eventually, Leo put his feet up on the chair in front of him and slouched down. It wasn't long before gentle snores were heard from his area.

Emily followed his lead and soon was also asleep. I couldn't help but notice that her head was resting on Leo's shoulder.

Time was passing slowly. We were afraid to talk for fear of scaring Ned and Nellie away. But sitting for so long in the deep darkness, it felt like we were in a cozy cave. There were no sounds other than the gentle snores of our younger team members. Soon those sounds were added to by the snorts of Tyler, and then Ethan succumbed as well.

"Should we stay here for the night?" Ollie whispered to Rachel and me.

"It's up to you," I said. "Wherever you are most comfortable. I don't think we're getting a show tonight. It's already two."

"Okay, gang. I'm going to head on back tonight," Rachel said.

"It's so late. Are you sure?" I asked.

"Yeah, it's not a long drive and I want to get in a full day tomorrow."

"Okay, be safe," I said as Ollie waved. We watched Rachel make her way through the doors of the lobby and not long after, we felt the air pressure shift as the front door opened and closed.

"I want to make sure we're locked up," I said, standing.

"I'll join you," Ollie said as she gathered blankets and pillows. I looked back to be sure the rest of the group was covered up, then followed her up the aisle.

Suddenly, a soft, eerie laughter echoed through the theater. The laughter was followed by hushed whispers, barely audible but unmistakable.

"You heard that, right?" Ollie asked.

"Yes," I whispered. "Let's sit back down."

We scooted into the seats closest to us and waited.

Another peal of laughter, this time louder, rang through the auditorium. We could see movement from the rest of the team in the rows ahead. They were waking up and stretching.

Another round of laughter had everyone sitting upright now and looking around. Tyler turned and saw us in the back. He waved.

Suddenly, the theater lights flickered on, casting a warm, golden glow over the room.

On stage, two ghostly figures appeared, dressed in early 20th-century vaudevillian attire. It was Ned and Nellie Harper.

Ned appeared as a tall, lanky man with a neatly combed mustache and slicked-back hair. He wore a pinstripe suit with a bowler hat and shiny shoes. He waggled his eyebrows up and down at the audience while Nellie smiled. She shimmied around the stage, making her flapper dress shimmer, and twirled her long sting of pearls in a large circle.

"Hey Nellie?"

"Yes, Ned?" She turned her large eyes on him as she patted down her bob.

"Why did the scarecrow become a successful actor?"

"Why, I have no idea Ned. Why did the scarecrow become a successful actor?"

"Because he was outstanding in his field!"

The team laughed as the joke was followed immediately by a stinger.

Ba-dum-tss!

"Where did that come from?" Ollie whispered.

I just shook my head.

"Hey, Ned?"

"Yes, Nellie?"

"Why don't you ever take me out to eat?" Nellie pouted.

"Why, I had plans to take you to the greatest restaurant ever. It's on the moon!"

"Oh, that sounds divine. How's the food?"

"It's out of this world, but there's no atmosphere."

Ba-dum-tss!

Music began playing, and soon, Ned and Nellie were dancing to a ragtime tune. Gabby whistled along.

The upbeat music completely woke us all up, and we began clapping along to the beat as Nellie's sparkly pumps moved rapidly around the stage. Mostly Ned stood still and played the klutz to her gracefulness.

When they finished, they held hands and bowed.

"Hey, Ned?"

"Yes, Nellie?"

"Why don't you take me out dancing more often?"

"Well, I would, but every time we go, people throw money at my feet. I'm afraid all those tips will make me trip."

"Oh, Neddie! With your moves, they are paying you to stop dancing."

Ba-dum-tss!

"Thank you, folks! It's been a pleasure performing for you tonight," Ned said.

"And remember, laughter is the best medicine. Even for ghosts!" Nellie added.

We all stood and applauded. Then, with a final bow, Ned and Nellie's forms faded, their laughter lingering in the air. The stage lights dimmed, returning the room to its previous state of gentle decay.

"Tell me we got that," I asked Leo as we practically ran back into the lobby.

TYLER REED: TAKE 2

" Good evening, viewers. I'm Tyler Reed, and welcome back to another thrilling episode of 'Haunted Histories.' Tonight, we're taking you inside Hawthorne Hall, a theater with a history as dark as its shadowy corridors. This grand old venue was once the cultural heartbeat of the town, hosting operas, plays, and concerts that drew the elite from miles around. But all that changed one fateful night when a devastating fire claimed the lives of its brightest stars, Ned and Nellie Harper."

The scene transitions to the dimly lit interior of the theater. Dust motes dance in the thin beams of light filtering through the grime-covered windows. The camera pans over the cracked marble floors and the tattered velvet curtains that once framed the stage.

"Local legend has it that the spirits of Ned and

Nellie Harper still haunt these halls, replaying their final performance for an audience that has long since passed on. But was the fire that ended their lives truly an accident, as the official reports claim? Or was it something far more sinister? Whispers of arson, jealousy, and a long-standing rivalry have plagued this theater ever since that tragic night."

The camera cuts to a close-up of Tyler standing in the middle of the stage, his expression serious and contemplative.

"Tonight, our team is here to uncover the truth. We aim to separate fact from fiction, and perhaps bring peace to the restless spirits that are said to roam this historic venue. We'll explore the mysterious sightings, the unexplained cold spots, and the eerie laughter that echoes through the empty halls. But more than that, we'll dig into the dark past of this theater to find out if the Harper's deaths were truly accidental or if there's a deeper mystery that has yet to be unraveled."

The camera transitions to the team, setting up their equipment in the theater's backstage area. Their faces are lit by the glow of their monitors as they prepare for the night ahead.

"Already, we've encountered strange phenomena—disembodied voices, flickering lights, and shadows that seem to move on their own. Could these be the lingering spirits of Ned and Nellie, or is there something else at play? Join us as we delve into the haunting history of Hawthorne Hall and find out for yourself, will we lay these spirits to rest, or will their tragic tale remain an unsolved mystery?"

The screen fades to black.

CHAPTER 6

Everyone buzzed with excitement as we elbowed each other out of the way to see what Leo had on his screen.

I prayed he was able to record Ned and Nellie on camera and whispered, "Please, please, please," as his fingers worked over buttons and keys.

Leo grinned, but his focus remained on the monitors. "Give me a second. I'm checking."

"Give it up," Ollie teased. "You know we didn't get it. We never do!"

"Olivia!" I exclaimed. "Try to be positive."

"Yeah, she's probably right." Tyler chimed in. "It's like a rule in paranormal shows. The cast sees something amazing and reacts, but to the audience there's nada."

"They are right," Ethan added. "If we actually

got anything usable, it would be a first," Ethan added, his eyes gleaming with anticipation.

"Still, you guys. Don't jinx us," Emily came to my defense as she rested an encouraging hand on Leo's shoulder. "And I like how negative everyone is being, yet you are all hovering over Leo like -"

"Wait!" Leo exclaimed. "Hang on... I think... yes! Look at this!" He pointed to the screen, and we all leaned in closer.

There, in the grainy footage, were the ghostly figures of Ned and Nellie Harper, performing their vaudeville routine. The image flickered and wavered, but it was unmistakable. The team erupted in cheers.

"Oh, my gosh! We got it! We actually got it!" Emily exclaimed, bouncing on her toes.

"This is incredible," Ethan said, shaking his head in disbelief. "We've never captured anything like this before."

"No one has," Leo said. "This is a first!"

I felt a mix of relief and exhilaration. "This is exactly what we needed. But do you guys think it's convincing? How will it play on TV?"

"There's always skepticism, you know," Leo said.

"But this is as good as I've ever seen," Tyler added.

"I might be able to do a little more, but not too much. The more I mess around with it, the more it will look like it was altered. That's worse. That would bring the skeptics out in full force."

As everyone agreed and watched Leo work his magic, something occurred to me. "Hey, Leo, speaking of messing around, can I ask you something now that Rachel has left?"

"Sure, what's up?" Leo asked, eyes still on the monitor.

"Well, I think we're all sort of curious about this. Earlier, when we were playing Two Truths and a Lie, were those really two truths?"

Leo smiled and turned towards me. "No," he said. "I wasn't joking around. I told two truths and one lie. Why?"

"Um, well, buddy," Ollie started. "What you shared was sort of surprising. I mean, there's got to be a story behind it all."

"Oh, there is," Leo started laughing.

I looked at Ollie and shrugged.

"Okay, you. Let us in on the gag," Ollie said.

Leo grew more serious and said, "I just didn't want to play that game. It was dumb. So I said what I thought would make the game end quickly. And it worked. None of it was true. Was that okay?"

We all laughed now and Ollie quickly added, "Oh, yes. That was certainly okay. You saved us all!"

It wasn't much longer before Leo finally finished what he was working on and shut down the equipment. I watched him turn off the small light he was using, and the lobby sank into darkness. After the excitement of seeing Ned and Nellie and then actually getting it on camera, I know everyone was exhausted. Gabby was on her perch just to my right and soon her gentle breaths were added to the soft snores that surrounded me.

It took a few more minutes, but my mind shut down and I was just beginning to drift to sleep.

"Fire! Fire!"

I bolted upright, my heart pounding. "What is it, Gabby?" I asked, but the smell of smoke hit me immediately. "Oh, no."

"Fire! Fire!" Gabby repeated, more insistent and even louder this time. Then she began making a noise like a firetruck siren, which quickly woke everyone up.

"Everyone!" I said, loudly. "Wake up!"

Ollie groaned, rolling over. "Gabby, what is that noise?"

"Smoke. I smell smoke," I said, my voice growing urgent.

Ollie sat up, sniffing the air. Her eyes widened. "Oh no. You're right. I smell it too."

"Guys, get up," she began nudging everyone as she gathered her equipment.

"I'll call 911," Ethan said.

"It's in here," Leo said as he opened the doors to the theater itself. Smoke poured into the lobby and he slammed the doors shut.

"Okay, you guys grab what you can and get out of the building," I said, preparing to be the last one out.

"We're okay," Ollie said. "It's in the theater part."

"Not in this building. We aren't okay," Ethan huffed as he slung bags over his shoulders. "So old and dry, it could go up like that." He paused long enough to snap his fingers.

We grabbed our essentials, making sure not to leave anything important behind. The smell of smoke grew stronger. We could see the faint glow of flames through the narrow windows in the theater doors.

"Stay together," I said, trying to keep my voice steady.

I heard fire trucks almost as soon as we stepped foot in the parking lot.

Gabby squawked again, "Fire! Fire!" And made her siren sound just to be sure we all knew.

"Thanks, Gabby," I muttered. "Just stay with me."

Thankfully, we didn't see flames spreading and

by the time the fire department arrived; it appeared no actual damage had been done.

"Looks like mostly smoke," the Chief said. "Seems someone started a fire in a barrel. Probably just to scare you, but not do any real damage."

A police officer had arrived by then and started asking questions. "Any idea who might have done this?"

We all shook our heads, but of course, there were plenty of people who might have done this.

"There's always someone who doesn't like what we do," I said.

"Right," Ollie added. "People who think we are playing around with evil or something like that and want us to leave."

"There are also business reasons," Tyler added. "Like the guy who wants to buy the place."

"Yeah, but why would he want us out of here?' Emily asked. "What does setting a fire that wouldn't actually burn down the theater solve? If he did burn it down, I could see that. But just running us off? Why?"

"I'll look into it," the officer said as he shook my hand. "Obviously, it was arson, even if nothing was destroyed. You folks need to be extra careful. In fact, I'm tempted to have you leave for the night."

"Oh, no, that's not necessary." We turned to see

Amanda Kerrigan. She reached out a hand to the officers and explained who she was.

"Mr. Hargrove is invested in having them here. He wants to maintain good relations with the community and the Haunted Histories crew is helping with that. Helping document the history of the place. It'll be a great remembrance for when he does buy it and then, well, you know, tears it down."

She smiled at each of us in turn as the officers nodded. "Okay, then you can stay if the owner is okay with that. But you need to keep watch and make sure the place is locked up tight. Next time, you might not be so lucky."

"Mr. Hargrove thanks you," Amanda said as they turned to leave.

We began walking towards the theater while Amanda continued to talk to the police. Once out of earshot, Ollie said, "What the heck was that?"

"I don't know," I said. "But I sure didn't like it. I thought she was on our side."

"Right, and he doesn't own the place. She said he's the owner," Leo added.

"Let's ask her what's going on," Emily said. She was bouncing again like a boxer ready for a fight.

"I will," I said. "Let me handle it, okay?"

With a lot of grumbling and muttering, the team once again set up in the lobby. As we all dragged various pieces of equipment back in, I glanced up and saw Amanda. She crooked her finger at me.

I joined her, and we walked away from the group.

"I think you have some thoughts," she said.

"Well, yes. I thought you were here to help us out. And after what you said to the police…"

As my words trailed off, she nodded.

"You are right. But you have to realize I was using Mr. Hargrove's name. He's so influential around here that he gets pretty much anything he wants. And if the cops thought he wanted you guys to stay here, that's what was going to happen," she paused, then took a deep breath. "Look, I don't really care one way or the other what happens to this place. My paycheck is the same no matter what. But I do think it's important that you all either prove this place is haunted and can attach some historical significance to it or not. Then Laura Bennett at the historical society, all those people, Mr. Hargrove, me, even you all, can then move on with our lives. You just got here, but this has had our town split for quite a long time."

I nodded as she spoke.

"Okay, I guess I can see where you're coming from."

"So, try to get some rest. It doesn't look like you've slept a wink all night long and it's almost morning already. I'll be back later this afternoon and we can talk some more if you'd like. Before I leave, I want to walk around and double-check all the doors to confirm they are locked. I'll leave out the back, though, so you need to make sure this front entrance is locked as well."

I stared dumbly at her back and wondered if Rachel had really locked the door behind her when she left. I kicked myself for not checking.

CHAPTER 7

"Oh, no! No no no no no nooooooo!"

"What's wrong, Leo?" Emily asked, springing out of her sleeping bag much faster than the rest of us.

"The video of Ned and Nellie, it's gone!"

"How is it gone?" I asked, thinking that it wasn't like back in the day when there was an actual VHS tape that could go missing. "Isn't it on a drive somewhere? Backed up and stuff?"

I know my technical side was showing, but Leo was gracious and explained that he hadn't had a chance to back it up and it was the actual laptop that had been taken.

"I was so stupid. I wanted to do more work on it and I guess I was tired and not thinking. I'm so sorry, you guys," he sobbed.

"Wait, you're saying someone stole your computer?" I asked incredulously.

"Yeah. We brought everything in and got the cameras set up again, but I didn't see my laptop. I figured it was in that bag with all the other ones. I just now got a really bad feeling and decided to look for it. It's gone."

"How is it that it's not on anything else?" Ollie asked. "With all this equipment, there's no way it's not recorded somewhere else. We always have backups in place." She put a comforting arm around his shoulders. "Come on, I'll help you look."

The two of them began going through everything they knew to do while the rest of us watched helplessly.

In frustration, I stood up.

"I need some fresh air," I said. "I'll be outside. I'm going to look for the laptop. Maybe it just was misplaced and is literally laying in the parking lot."

No one really thought that was the case, but they knew I needed to be alone for a while.

As Gabby and I squinted in the early morning sun, I did look around the lot. You never knew. Still, I didn't have a feeling about it and was pretty sure I wouldn't find anything. Regardless, the real reason for my solace was to think.

I was slowly but surely learning to listen to my

gut when it told me I needed to do something and right now, it told me that something was going on. Of course, whoever started the fire was a pretty major issue that needed to be addressed. But even beyond that, Amanda was strange. What was it she said? Something about us proving one way or another if the theater was haunted. And she made that comment just hours after we did indeed do that.

But how could she have known? She wasn't with us. Did she have hidden cameras in the theater? Or even just security cameras?

I didn't think so. Those types of things tended to affect Leo's, and especially Ollie's, equipment. One of them would have said something and gone looking for the culprit.

"She did show up awfully fast," Gabby said.

I hadn't realized I was talking to myself and Gabby responded to my last comment.

Wait! Gabby responded to my last comment.

"Gabby?" I said slowly. "You're doing it again."

Just like at the mansion, Gabby was speaking in complete sentences and using words that she didn't normally use.

Rather than answer me, she simply turned her big black eyes on me, then she cocked her head to the side.

"All right, I get it," I said. "She did show up awfully fast. You are correct. Almost as though she knew something was going to happen, and she was ready to be here. Do you think she started the fire?"

"You know, it's a good thing I love you." Ollie's voice made me jump. I had been waiting for Gabby to respond.

"What?" I blurted.

"Well, you're out here talking to Gabby. No offense, Gabs, like she's a person. I swear you are expecting her to answer you." Ollie laughed and ran a hand down Gabby's back.

I laughed too, but not as convincingly. Having known me for so long gave Ollie a sort of super-power where my lies were concerned. She called me out on this one too.

"Sis, what's going on?" She asked.

"Ollie, you're going to think I've completely lost it, but Gabby does answer me."

"Well, that's normal. Gabby is extremely intelligent and-,"

I shook my head. "No, not normal."

"Okay...that's okay. So are you saying she's talking to you differently? Like with actual words? Or, uh, are they maybe words you hear in your head?"

I could tell she was trying to be sensitive to my unique senses and psychic ability while also wondering if I had officially lost my mind.

"Actual words," I grumbled. "Like you and me

right now. Full sentences. Gabby, could you, maybe? For me? Say something to Ollie?"

Gabby turned her dark eyes on Ollie and me. After an exaggerated pause, she said, "Polly wanna cracker?"

Ollie busted out with laughter. "I've never ever heard her say that! Gabby, are you learning new words? That's great! Okay, you're off the hook."

I laughed along with Ollie and Gabby, even made her clicking sound that she used to show happiness.

"I was just checking on you out here. It seems you're okay. I'll leave you two to it, then. Let us know what you come up with. The team is sorta stuck right now, and they sent me out here to make sure you aren't stuck, too. We need our fearless leader."

"Yeah, okay. Thanks," I said. "I'll be back inside in a minute."

When Ollie was out of earshot, I whispered to Gabby. "That was mean."

Gabby lowered her voice and whispered back, "I know."

I strode back into the theater and stopped with my hands on my hips.

I cleared my throat, and when everyone was looking at me, I spoke.

"First, we need to talk to Amanda. I don't think she should be here anymore, especially alone. I'm pretty sure she started the fire."

My thoughts were met with solemn nods. Apparently, my announcement wasn't very original and everyone agreed.

"Second, we have to get into the passageways under the theater today. As soon as possible. We have to see if we can find that evil room Margaret was talking about yesterday. Even if there isn't anything there of a supernatural sort, I'll bet we find something. They did say it had been closed off for a long time, right?"

"Yes, the section where Ned and Nellie died. It's boarded up," Ethan said. "And you are not going alone. I'll go with you."

"Actually, I want to go too," Leo said. "And really, I should with the camera."

"I'll go too," Ollie said. "Same reason, but with audio. We know sometimes we can hear more than we can see."

"Right, and me too, you know, in case there's something to report on or interview, or something," Tyler said.

"You sort of lost it there at the end, Tyler," Emily laughed. "Are you going to interview ghosts now?"

There were a few nervous chuckles, then Emily added, "But yeah, me too. Let's go ghost hunting. With all of us there, what could possible go wrong?"

~

Oh dear, sweet Emily. Never ever ask a question like that because as soon as you do, you will get your answer.

Feeling like we'd already been jinxed, our tight-knit group made its way onto the stage and around into the wings of the theater. It was dark and musty, but we'd brought our flashlights. Unfortunately, all they illuminated were the spider webs and dust motes that floated in the air.

I consulted the map I'd made to help us find the boarded up area where Ned and Nellie died. It was down several hallways that led us even deeper into the bowels of the theater, far beyond the manager's office. I wondered if this was the same passageway that was rumored to be evil. It didn't seem likely that the place where Ned and Nellie died would be designated that way.

Dust clung to the damp walls, and our footsteps echoed faintly off the wooden floors. The team was unusually quiet, the weight of our mission pressing down on us. We knew we were venturing into uncharted territory—both physically and, perhaps, paranormally.

Gabby shifted uneasily on my shoulder, her claws digging into my jacket. I couldn't blame her; the atmosphere was tense, and even I was on edge. This part of the theater had been sealed off for decades, forgotten by everyone except the ghosts— or whatever else might be down here.

Ollie was close behind, adjusting her audio equipment as we moved. "This place gives me the creeps," she muttered, more to herself than to anyone else. "But if there's anything to catch, this is where we'll find it."

"That's the spirit," I said.

The further we went, the more I could feel... something. It was like an itch at the back of my mind, a tingling sensation that told me we were getting closer to whatever secrets this place held.

Finally, we reached the end of the hallway, where boards were crisscrossed over a large opening. Ethan paused, shining his light over the rotted wood that led to who knew what. "This has to be it," he said, his voice barely above a whisper. "The area where Ned and Nellie died."

"Do we really want to go in there?" Emily's voice was shaky, and I could see the nervous anticipation in her eyes.

"We have to," I replied, taking a deep breath. "This is where we start. And guys," I decided to be completely honest. "I'm having some really strong feelings here. There is evil in this area. I just know it. Something more than it just being old and abandoned. Something is here."

"Way to bury the lede," Ollie muttered as she and Leo pushed past me.

"Let's get whatever this is on record," Leo added.

Ethan and Tyler easily pulled the crumbling and rotting boards away from the wall. Between the damp and the termites, the planks broke apart and splintered easily.

A whiff of stale air snaked out of the hole, thick with the scent of mildew and something else.

We climbed our way through the hole, careful to avoid splinters and cobwebs, and found ourselves inside a room that was large and empty, except for the remnants of old stage props and costumes strewn across the floor. The walls were blackened with soot, a stark reminder of the fire that had claimed two lives so many years ago. The oppressive feeling intensified as we stepped inside, as if the room itself was holding its breath, waiting for something.

Gabby suddenly flapped her wings, startling all of us. "I see dead people!" she squawked, her voice unnervingly loud in the confined space.

"Gabby, not now," I whispered, trying to calm her, but my heart was racing.

Ethan moved further into the room, his flashlight sweeping across the floor. "What do you feel, Jackie?"

"Gabby is right. There's something here," I said. "Be careful."

"Look over here," Ollie called out, pointing her light toward a corner of the room. Another set of boards haphazardly crisscrossed the wall.

"Is it another entrance?" Emily asked.

We all gathered around as Ethan and Tyler once again pried boards and planks from the wall in a cascade of rotten wood and splinters.

"Looks like another room," Leo said, adjusting the camera to get a better angle. "But why would it be boarded up too?"

We took turns holding flashlights while we each helped the other duck and creep into the small room that was just off of Ned and Nellie's dressing room. It was equally empty, with the exception of a large piece of furniture covered by an old, dusty blanket. And something was in the middle of the floor.

Tyler bent over and picked it up carefully. "The Final Act," he read.

"What is it?" Emily asked, craning her neck to see.

"Looks like a script," Tyler said, his voice barely above a whisper.

"Let's take it with us and get out of this part of

the room," I said. "I'm not at all comfortable. Something bad is going to happen."

No one argued, and we quickly filed back through the hole. Back in the first room, the lights on our equipment flickered, and a cold gust of wind blew through, despite there being no visible source. Gabby squawked loudly, and suddenly, the room was filled with the faint sound of laughter— Ned and Nellie's voices, echoing through the darkness.

TYLER REED: TAKE 3

The camera opens with a panoramic view of Hawthorne Hall, shrouded in the early morning mist. The scene transitions to the charred remains of the theater's interior, where the team stands amidst the ruins, their faces lit by the faint glow of their flashlights.

"Good evening, everyone. I'm Tyler Reed, and welcome back to 'Haunted Histories.' Tonight, we continue our investigation into Hawthorne Hall—a place where the echoes of the past refuse to fade. What began as a simple exploration of this abandoned theater has quickly escalated into a chilling discovery."

"Our cameras have captured something extraordinary—the ghostly figures of Ned and Nellie Harper, performing their final act in this very theater. But just as we began to unravel this mystery, someone—or something—tried to stop us. A fire broke out, forcing us to evacuate. And our footage was stollen. Was this an attempt to drive us away? Or was it a warning from beyond the grave?"

The scene transitions to the team cautiously re-entering the theater, now filled with the acrid smell of smoke. The camera follows as they descend into the darkened passageways beneath the stage.

"Despite the dangers, we pressed on, determined to uncover the secrets hidden within these walls. What we found was more than we ever expected—an old, forgotten room sealed off for decades. The air was thick with the scent of mildew and something far more sinister. It was here, in this forsaken space, that we discovered an ominous artifact—a charred book, its pages filled with a script titled, 'The Final Act.'"

The camera zooms in on the book, its blackened cover barely legible in the dim light.

"But why was this room sealed away? What secrets does this script hold? And could it be the key to understanding the tragic events that took place here so many years ago? As we delve deeper into Hawthorne Hall's dark history, we must tread carefully. The forces at play are growing stronger, and the line between the living and the dead is becoming dangerously thin."

The camera cuts back to Tyler, his expression somber as he stands at the entrance of the sealed room.

"Join us as we continue to explore the mysteries of Hawthorne Hall. With every step we take, the past becomes more entwined with the present. But one thing is certain—Hawthorne Hall is a place where the final act is never truly over."

CHAPTER 8

Ned and Nellie appeared before us, their forms appearing as though we could touch them. Although none of us wanted to. They wore the same costumes they had on last night and looked the exact same. The only exception was their smiles were replaced with worry.

"Are you our audience from last night?" Nellie asked.

We all nodded and I could see Tyler swallow hard before croaking out, "Yes, ma'am."

His manners greatly improved when speaking to a ghost.

"We are happy to have you here," Ned added. "But why are you down here? In our dressing room?"

"Right, and for the love of two left feet, why did

you open that door?" Nellie asked as she pointed to the room we had just left.

"Oh yeah, boy. You opened up a whole can of worms with that one," Ned said.

"What do you mean?" I asked. "What did we do?"

"That's Franklin's dressing room," Nellie whispered. "We've managed to keep him in there all this time, but now that the door was opened, I'm not sure we'll be able to manage it any longer. He's an angry man, right Neddie?"

Ned nodded slowly and put a protective arm around Nellie.

"Indeed, darling," he muttered.

"What do you think he might do?" Tyler asked.

"Yes, why do you say he's angry? What happened?" Ethan added his questions.

I wondered if Ned and Nellie knew of the rumors that Franklin had started the fire that apparently killed them all. Or if they hadn't heard the rumors, if they knew for sure that he did.

"He just didn't play fair," Nellie said.

"He was always fighting with someone," Ned added.

"He wanted to be the top banana," Nellie added.

It didn't seem as though they knew, and if they did, they weren't saying anything.

When a gust of cold air went through the room, we all shivered and Ned and Nellie's forms flickered in the breeze.

"What was that?" Emily asked.

"Franklin," Ned said. "Look, you folks seem nice enough, but you've opened up a whole can of worms here. And I'm afraid it might be dangerous for you to stick around the place. We'll try to get Franklin tucked up into his room again, but just in case we can't...,"

"Well, just in case, you should go on and leave. And please do let the others know to wait a bit before they come for another show. We don't want anyone else to get hurt," Nellie added.

Then they both disappeared.

Just as we breathed a sigh of relief, another cold gust blew through the room and yet another figure appeared before us. There was no mistaking who it was. We stood face to face with Franklin Mason.

"Oh, drat, I just missed the lovely couple," he said as he twirled his Snidely Whiplash mustache and adjusted his monocle.

"Tell you what, I'll save you some trouble," he said as he flipped the tails of his coat. "Yes, I started the fire that killed the precious Harpers. And yes, I got trapped as well and I died. We are all tied to this place, but those nitwits don't seem to realize it.

They just keep on showing off like they always have, playing their shows and tripping along as though nothing has happened. I know, though. I know what happened. And now that I'm free, I'm going to be the star again."

He twirled again and the tails of his coat flew through the air, stirring up dust and dirt all around.

I tried hard, but I simply couldn't suppress a sneeze. Then Tyler sneezed. Then Leo and Emily. Ethan was holding his arm over his nose while his eyes watered. Ollie had her nose pinched tight.

Franklin's ghost watched us in our fits of allergies, and with each sneeze, he grew angrier and angrier.

"Stop it!" He demanded. "Stop that immediately. I deserve reverence, not this display. Stop it!"

We tried as hard as we could, but each time he yelled "stop it" he flung his coat tails even more and by now the dust was flying all over. It got worse, and we began to cough.

"This is unacceptable. Get out! Leave now! Leave before I make you leave." He threw his hands in the air and made himself appear even larger than before.

He didn't have to ask us twice, though. As quickly as possible, we all rushed for the small space and in a farce that would have done Ned and Nellie proud, we all hit the opening at the same time and bounced backwards. Then the show continued as the men stepped back and gestured for the women to go first, but Ollie was still recording and wanted to be one of the last out with Leo, and I was determined no one would be injured so I refused as well. We all stood looking at each other while Franklin continued to rant and rave about our lack of intelligence.

Then Emily finally went through. She paused on the other side to confirm that everyone else was coming, which only made Ethan and Tyler run into her.

I had stepped back by now and was watching the fiasco from a distance. I tried not to look, but I could see Franklin glaring at the group. His anger was wild and intense. At the same time, and in direct conflict with what I saw, I heard the faint sounds of giggling.

On the other side of the room, Ned and Nellie were holding their stomachs and doubled over with laughter.

A quick glance back to Franklin and I knew everything I needed to know. Not only was he upstaged by the Harpers, he was now being upstaged by a group of talentless ordinary, and according to him, unintelligent people.

Franklin raised his hand as though he were going to strike someone just before Leo reached back through the opening and dragged me through.

We held hands as we ran back down the hallway. Emily had picked up the map and held it in front of her as we ran. She navigated the twists and turns and got us back to the lobby in one piece.

For a moment, no one spoke. We were all too stunned, too shaken by what we'd just witnessed. Then Gabby, who had been unusually quiet, broke the silence.

"That was a hoot!" She said.

"Yeah, it was pretty funny," Ollie agreed. "When we all just stood there waiting for someone to go!"

"And then we all went at the same time," Emily added.

"Ned and Nellie were amused. Did you all see them? They were watching and laughing at our little show," I added.

"Really? Shucks, I missed that," Ethan said.

"It was funny, you guys, but on a serious note, this just got a lot more complicated."

"Yeah," I agreed. "But at least we know what we're up against now. Franklin Mason... We need to find out what's keeping him here and end it."

Ethan nodded, his expression grim. "Agreed.

We have to be smart about this. If he's as dangerous as Ned and Nellie say, we can't afford to take any chances."

"I think we got away with it this time, but if, or when, we encounter him again, we won't be so lucky. And I don't think Ned and Nellie can help us," I said to solemn nods all around. "Okay, everyone, I think we all know what we need to do. Let's see what we can find and figure out what ties Franklin to this place. Obviously, he died here just like Ned and Nellie, but why didn't he cross over when he died?"

"And for that matter," Ethan said, "why didn't Ned and Nellie?"

That was a good question, but no one had a good answer.

"What do you think will happen to Ned and Nellie if the theater is destroyed?" Tyler asked.

"Most likely, they would be destroyed too," Leo whispered.

With heavy hearts, everyone drifted to the bathrooms to get cleaned up. I still couldn't shake the feeling that we were running out of time. Now that Franklin knew we were here, and based on what we just witnessed, he wouldn't just sit back and let us uncover his secrets. I had to keep everyone focused, but I also needed to keep them safe.

Ollie came back first and plopped down in one

of the lobby chairs with an old newspaper. I moved next to her.

"Anything interesting?"

"Plenty. But nothing good. Franklin wasn't just jealous of Ned and Nellie. It seems he was obsessed with them. These articles paint a picture of a man who was constantly in their shadow, desperate for recognition."

She opened her laptop and pulled up an image of a yellowed article from the local paper, dated a few months before the fire. The headline read: *"Franklin Mason: The Forgotten Actor?"* The article went on to detail Franklin's growing frustration with being overshadowed by the more popular duo, hinting at a rivalry that was anything but friendly.

By now the rest of the team was back, and Ollie got their attention.

"Listen to this, guys," she said, reading aloud from the article. "Franklin Mason, once a rising star in the local theater scene, has struggled to maintain his former glory. With the Harper duo consistently taking center stage, Mason has found himself relegated to supporting roles—a situation that sources say has led to increasing tension behind the scenes."

I frowned, the pieces starting to come together. "So Franklin wasn't just jealous—he felt like he was being pushed aside."

"Right. That would explain his anger, but it doesn't explain why he's still here. There has to be something more," Emily added.

Ollie nodded, scrolling through more images. "There's definitely something more. Listen to this. *'Tragic Fire Claims Two Lives at Hawthorne Hall,'* is the headline."

I jumped in. "Here's the last paragraph. 'While the cause of the fire remains undetermined, rumors have surfaced, suggesting that the fire may have been intentionally set. Some have speculated that Franklin Mason, who was present that night, might have been involved, though no evidence has been found to support these claims.'"

"So they suspected Franklin, even back then," Ethan said.

"But they couldn't prove it," Ollie finished, her voice low. "And with him disappearing after the fire, it only added to the mystery."

"Wouldn't they have found his body, too?" Emily looked up and asked.

"Or did they overlook his death as well as his life?" Leo said.

Sitting quietly with all that entailed, we continued to search when Tyler spoke up.

"Hey everyone, I think I found something here. It's was folded up in the back of the script for 'The Final Act.' Listen, 'I can no longer stand by and watch as Ned and Nellie Harper steal the spotlight that is rightfully mine. I have given everything to this theater, but it is clear that my efforts will never be recognized as long as they are here. I am leaving, but not before I ensure that the world remembers the name Franklin Mason. They will all see that I was the true star, not those two charlatans.'"

A heavy silence fell over the room as the implications of the letter sank in.

"What does that mean?" Emily asked.

"He was planning something," Leo said, his voice grim. "He didn't just want to leave or resign. He wanted to go out with a bang and be remembered."

"And he did," I added, the pieces finally clicking into place. "He started the fire to make sure Ned and Nellie wouldn't outshine him anymore. But something must have gone wrong."

"I hate to be a broken record, but I have to ask again. Why is he still here?" Ethan asked.

"Could there be some item he's tied to? Something other than the theater itself, of course. Is there something personal of his?" Ollie wondered.

"Well, yeah, the script," Tyler said, waving the document in the air. "But we can't destroy it. Right? We shouldn't destroy this."

"No, I don't think that's the thing to do." I walked to Tyler and put my hand on his shoulder. "It doesn't feel right to do that. Are we all agreed?"

Everyone nodded solemnly.

"We agree on that, but can we agree on what our next steps are?" This time, everyone just looked at me. No one had any ideas.

Except Ethan, who was turning an odd shade of pink.

Then he cleared his throat and whispered. "We could call Clara."

CHAPTER 9

"She's here! Everyone, she's here. I'll go get her."

Ethan sort of skipped through the lobby when Clara arrived. He stopped just short of the doors when Emily took his arm and pulled him to her. She straightened his shirt collar and then reached up and patted a stray hair into place.

Looking handsome and put together, he rushed through the doors, only to return a few moments later with Clara on his arm. In his other hand, he held her small bag.

"Be cool everyone," Ollie whispered. But it was fruitless. The oohs and aahs from the group made both of them blush.

"Okay, okay," Ethan said. "It's true. We've been seeing each other a bit."

"No! You're kidding?" Tyler exclaimed.

"Yes, just a few dates here and there," she smiled up at Ethan, who turned even redder and again had to clear his throat to speak.

"I'll let you get started. I'll put your bag over here, next to my cot."

Emily started to make another 'ooh' sound, but a sharp look from Ollie stopped her quickly.

"It's so great to see you," I said as I hugged Clara tight.

"You, too, dear," she said. "Come, let's walk around a little. I'd like to see this place for myself."

I tapped my shoulder and Gabby flew to it as I led Clara into the theater itself.

"We've been digging into the past, but so far, it's just given us more questions than answers," I said.

"What is your instinct telling you?" Clara asked.

"Nothing really. I tried to use it the other day. Did Ethan tell you about Leo's computer being stolen?"

Clara nodded.

"I hoped to find it was just overlooked or something, but nothing happened."

I glanced quickly at Gabby, still perched on my shoulder, remembering how she had spoken to me in full sentences that day and refused to do it for Ollie. I wondered if she would do it again for Clara.

"So just that one time? And nothing

happened? Nothing at all?" Clara asked. She stopped walking and looked from me to Gabby and then back at me.

Was it possible she knew?

Clara kept looking between the two of us, and it was becoming uncomfortable. Feeling as though I had nothing to lose, I said, "Gabby thinks Amanda might have something to do with it."

Clara smile. "Gabby is probably correct. Tell me more about Amanda and her role here."

We continued walking, and I filled her in on Amanda Kerrigan and Richard Hargrove and their confusing interest in the theater. "I mean, I get Hargrove. He wants the money from tearing it down and doing whatever he wants to do. But Amanda? Why is she so invested? If she didn't care at all, she would just do her job, but for her to show up the night of the fire in the barrel, and then keep showing up in strange places..." I let my voice trail off.

"Again, I ask you, what does your instinct say?"

"Amanda did show up very quickly that night. I suppose it's possible she started the fire, but honestly, I don't think she did. I think she really is on our side."

"Okay, go on," Clara prompted.

"I truly don't know about the laptop. I have no instincts or feelings at all."

"That's fine, dear. What else?"

"Well, there's Franklin. I'm convinced there's more to it than him being attached to the theater for some reason. I think that's why Ned and Nellie are here. I believe they are attached and I really think they need to stay. They want to stay. But Franklin ... there's just more to it. It's not as simple as destroying something of his, or finding his bones, or anything like that."

Clara smiled. "I think you're onto something there," she said. "It's more about what happened before the night of the fire."

"Yes! Franklin was so unhappy. He was being upstaged by Ned and Nellie, and he was so bitter. It was so important to him to be famous. Was his ego truly that big?"

"Let's find out," Gabby said.

"Yes, Gabby, let's," Clara said.

We were joined on stage by the rest of the team, frustrated and curious about being left out of the plans.

"We've found everything we can about the night of the fire, but we're still no closer," Emily groused.

"That's because Franklin's story isn't just about what happened the night of the fire," Clara explained, her voice steady. "It's about the years leading up to it—the rivalries, the broken dreams, and the obsession that drove him to do what he did."

Ollie shook her head. "It's always the backstory, isn't it? Ghosts are just like people—only more complicated."

We sat down on the stage where we were standing while we discussed what to do about Franklin. Leo and Ollie continued to record, and Tyler was making notes for his voice over.

Clara smiled slightly. "Exactly. And to understand Franklin, you need to understand what he wanted more than anything: to be remembered, to be seen as the star he believed he was."

"So how do we give him that without getting ourselves killed?" Leo asked, still adjusting his equipment as if the motion could help him process everything.

"I think Jackie knows."

Everyone turned expectant eyes on me and waited.

"I do?" I said. "I don't think I do, Clara. I mean, I had a few thoughts while we were talking, but nothing was clear. Not like a real plan or anything. Although, I guess we could do something to show Franklin that he's not forgotten. It must have something to do with that play, right? Tyler, who wrote the play?"

"Franklin Mason."

"Oh, well, then that's it. We have to perform the play and invite Franklin to be the star. And then we have to make sure he gets the credit for writing the play. Then he can rest easy. It's simple, really."

I smiled as five faces stared back, mouths agape.

Emily blinked. "You want us to perform a play for a ghost?"

"Well, no. I want someone to perform his play and I want him to be the star."

"But what about the audience? Won't we need more people?" Ethan asked.

"Nah," I said. "It'll be fine."

Slowly, Ollie began to nod. "Okay, okay, I think I can see this. Where do we start?"

"We start by understanding the script—the lines, the roles, everything. Once we know what we're dealing with, we can plan how to execute it."

Tyler opened the script and ran his fingers over the lettering. "This is going to be one for the record books," he muttered.

"The key will be drawing him to the stage," I said. "Any ideas?"

Leo sighed loud and dramatically.

"What?" I asked.

"You know we have to go back down there, right? We can't just summon him up here."

"He's right," a small voice whispered from just off the stage. We looked over to see Nellie peeking around the curtain. "There's a mirror in his dressing room. You need that."

She winked, then she was gone.

"Well, I like her a lot more than I did that other gal at Meadowbrook," Clara said, laughing. "Alrighty friends, let's go find a mirror and then we'll put on a show to end all shows."

"Well done with the psychic stuff, sis," Ollie whispered to me as we gathered items for our next trip to the basement. We were away from the group looking for extra batteries.

"Thank you. I think I just needed Clara to ask the right questions, you know?"

"I wish I could do that for you." Ollie shrugged. "I guess that's not for me to do, though. I still hope I help you. At least a little?"

I started to say that of course, Ollie helped. She was everything to me and would always be my best friend. How could she not be the most important person in my life after all she did for me when my sister went missing?

But before I could say anything, Gabby spoke up. "Ollie, you mean the world to both of us."

Ollie's mouth dropped open, and her eyes bugged out.

"Ha!" I said, jabbing my finger at her. "Told you."

"Slow your roll," Gabby admonished.

"Oh, my gosh."

Yelling 'ha' at Ollie seemed to get the attention of everyone else and they were watching us intently. Ollie quickly wiped away a tear, and then another one started down her face. She would have been mortified if anyone saw her crying, and I definitely didn't want to explain why.

I had to distract them.

"Are we ready? We need to go back down to his dressing room again." As I walked towards them, Gabby flew from my shoulder and landed on Ollie's. She fanned her wings and hid Ollie's face from the group.

"What's going on over there?" Emily asked as she motioned to Ollie and Gabby.

"Bonding, I guess," was the only answer I could come up with. "Anyway, the dressing room?"

"His dressing room, right?" Leo asked. "That smaller room off the larger room?"

I nodded. "I'll say it again. No one has to go down there. It's not safe and I won't have anyone harmed on my watch again. I'll go and I can take a camera with me and-,"

I was cut off by grunts and other noises from the group as everyone disagreed.

"No more talking about it. Let's go," Ethan said.

Ollie joined us and handed around the extra batteries. Emily looked at her curiously but didn't say anything else.

Gabby flew to my shoulder, and we began our march back under the stage.

"I feel like we're going into a lion's den," Tyler muttered, running a hand through his hair.

Leo, who had been uncharacteristically quiet, finally spoke up. "I just hope the equipment survives. I'm still not over losing my laptop."

As we descended further into the bowels of Hawthorne Hall once more, the air grew colder, the darkness deeper. And all the while, I could feel Franklin's presence growing stronger, like a weight pressing down on my chest.

"Stay close," I whispered, leading the way with my flashlight, cutting a narrow beam through the pitch-black tunnel. "And keep your eyes open. If Franklin tries anything, we need to be ready."

We moved slowly, cautiously, every step echoing in the darkness. The air was thick with dust and the scent of mildew, and the walls were damp to the touch.

As we approached the area that had been boarded up, we slowed down. Then, one by one, we climbed into the main room and gathered our wits. Ethan, ever the gentleman, offered his hand to Clara, who carefully picked her way through the splinters wearing her ballerina flats.

"I wore the wrong shoes for this," she muttered.

We paused in the larger room to give Clara an

opportunity to look around and for us to get our bearings and calm our nerves. After a few moments, we entered the smaller room.

In the center of the room stood a massive piece of furniture covered by a large, black velvet blanket. Clara reached out and flung the cover off, revealing an ornate mirror, its surface cracked and tarnished with age. The mirror was framed by twisted, blackened metal that looked like it had been forged in fire, and the glass itself seemed to shimmer with a strange, otherworldly light. It was as if the mirror was alive, pulsing with energy that radiated outwards, filling the room with an oppressive, suffocating presence.

"This must be what Nellie said we needed," Ethan said, his voice barely above a whisper as he approached the mirror.

I stepped closer, my heart pounding in my chest as I stared into the mirror. The reflections were distorted; the glass warped and cracked, but there was something in there—something moving just beneath the surface, like a shadow flickering in the depths.

"Be careful," I warned, reaching out to stop Ethan from getting too close. "We don't know what we're dealing with."

"Look," Emily said, her voice trembling as she pointed to the mirror. "I can see him... It's Franklin."

"We have to destroy it," Leo said, his voice firm. "If this mirror is what's keeping Franklin here, then we need to break it."

I opened my mouth to remind him we were going to move the mirror to the stage, not break it, but as soon as Leo spoke, the chamber seemed to come alive with a surge of energy. The air crackled with electricity, and the walls trembled as if the theater itself was protesting our presence.

"Get back!" I shouted, pulling Emily away from the mirror just as a deafening roar filled the chamber. The mirror's surface rippled like water, and a dark figure stepped out, solidifying into the twisted form of Franklin Mason.

His eyes glowed with a malevolent light, and his face was contorted in a mask of rage and hatred. The cartoonish image of Snidely Whiplash was gone. In its place stood the same figure, this time with a long black cape and a penetrating, evil stare.

"You dare to challenge me?" he hissed, his voice echoing through the chamber with a force that sent chills down my spine. "You came back despite my warnings."

The temperature in the chamber plummeted, and a fierce wind whipped through the room, pulling at our clothes and sending debris flying.

Franklin's spirit was more powerful here than anywhere else in the theater—this was his sanctuary, the place where he had hidden and grown stronger over the years.

"We have to fight him!" Ethan shouted over the roar of the wind. "This is our only chance!"

Leo raised the camera, capturing every terrifying moment as Franklin advanced on us, his eyes burning with fury. "We need to get him back into the mirror," he called out, his voice strained with effort. "It's the only way to trap him!"

But Franklin would not make it easy. He raised one hand, and the mirror behind him pulsed with dark energy. Shadows poured out of it, swirling around the chamber like a storm, obscuring our vision and making it impossible to see more than a few feet ahead.

"Don't let him separate us!" I yelled, grabbing Ollie's arm to keep her close. "We have to stay together!"

But even as I said it, the shadows grew thicker, more oppressive, closing in around us like a living, breathing entity. I could feel Franklin's presence all around me, his anger and hatred pressing down on my chest like a physical weight.

"Jackie!" Emily's voice called out from somewhere in the darkness, her tone filled with fear. "I can't see you!"

"Keep talking!" I shouted back, trying to make

my way through the swirling shadows. "We'll find you!"

But the darkness was too thick, the shadows too strong. I could hear the others calling out, their voices distorted and faint, as if they were miles away. Franklin's laughter echoed through the chamber, mocking us, taunting us as we struggled against the force of his power.

"Gabby!" I called out, hoping my loyal companion could help guide me through the darkness. But Gabby was silent.

And then, just as suddenly as it had started, the wind died down. The shadows receded, revealing Franklin standing in the center of the chamber, his form more solid, more real than ever before. He was drawing strength from the mirror, feeding off its energy, and with each passing moment, he grew more powerful.

"We're running out of time," Clara said, her voice tight with urgency. "If we don't act now, we'll lose our chance."

"But how do we stop him?" Ollie asked, her voice trembling. "He's too strong!"

I stared at the mirror, the centerpiece of Franklin's domain, and an idea formed in my mind. "We need to use the mirror against him," I said, the pieces of the puzzle finally clicking into place. "If he's drawing power from it, then maybe we can reverse it—trap him inside."

"But how?" Leo asked, his grip tightening on the camera as he tried to keep it steady. "How do we force him back into the mirror?"

"We have to weaken him first," I said, my mind racing. "Break his connection to the theater, to this place. We have to destroy whatever's left of his presence here—every trace of it."

Ethan nodded, his expression grim. "We'll have to do it together. It's the only way."

As we prepared to confront Franklin, I felt a surge of determination rise within me. We had come this far, faced unimaginable danger, and we would not back down now. Franklin might have had the upper hand, but we had something he didn't—the strength of our bonds, our trust in each other.

And we were going to use that strength to end this once and for all.

The air in Franklin's domain was thick with tension, each breath like inhaling ice shards. My heart pounded in my chest as I glanced around at my team, the faces of my friends reflecting the same mix of fear and determination I felt. We had come too far to back down now, even as the very walls of Hawthorne Hall seemed to pulse with Franklin's malevolent energy.

Franklin stood before the mirror, his form more solid than any ghost we'd ever encountered. He was almost tangible now, his twisted features contorted with a hatred that had festered for decades. The flickering light from the mirror cast eerie shadows across his face, making him look less like a man and more like a creature from a nightmare.

"You think you can take this from me?" Franklin hissed, his voice echoing through the chamber like the hiss of a snake. "I will not be forgotten!"

His words sent a chill down my spine, but I forced myself to stand tall, refusing to let him see my fear. "We're not here to take anything, Franklin," I said, keeping my voice steady. "We're here to end this. We want to give you your time."

Franklin's eyes burned with fury. "End this? You can't end this! My time is now! I am eternal! I am power!" His form seemed to swell with anger, the shadows around him growing darker, denser, as if feeding off his rage.

Leo stepped forward, his camera raised, capturing every moment.

"We know what you are, Franklin," Clara said, her voice calm despite the tension crackling in the air. "You're a ghost, a memory twisted by hate. But you don't have to stay here. You can move on."

"Move on?" Franklin spat the words like they were poison. "To what? Oblivion? No! I will not be erased! I will be remembered! I will have my revenge!"

Tyler tried to appeal to whatever humanity was left in Franklin's spirit. "Revenge isn't the answer, Franklin. It never was. I read your play. You were a great playwright and a great actor. People admired you, respected you. But holding onto this hatred is only destroying you."

Franklin's laugh was bitter and devoid of any warmth. "Admired? Respected? I was forgotten! Cast aside like a broken prop, while those charlatans, Ned and Nellie, took everything that should have been mine!"

He raised his hands, and the mirror behind him pulsed with a dark energy, the light within it growing brighter, more intense. The ground beneath us trembled, and I could feel the theater itself responding to Franklin's rage, the walls groaning as if they might collapse at any moment.

"We use his own power against him," I said, the idea crystallizing in my mind. "The mirror is the key—it's amplifying his energy, but it's also his anchor. If we can reflect that energy back at him, it might be enough to weaken him."

Leo nodded, already moving to adjust the angle of the camera. "We'll need something reflective—something to direct the energy away from us and back at the mirror."

Tyler began patting his pockets. "Here. It's not much, but you can try with my mirror."

"It'll have to do," I said, taking the mirror from

him. "Everyone, get ready. We need to time this perfectly."

As we spread out around the chamber, I looked at Gabby, her feathers ruffled and her eyes wide with fear. But she didn't leave my side.

Franklin's eyes narrowed as he watched us, his form growing more unstable, more monstrous, as he fed off the energy of the mirror. "You can't stop me," he growled, his voice echoing with the sound of cracking glass. "I am Hawthorne Hall. I am eternal!"

"No, Franklin," I said, raising the mirror and positioning it to catch the light from the larger mirror behind him. "You're just a ghost, and it's time to let go."

With a final, furious roar, Franklin hurled a blast of dark energy toward us, the force of it strong enough to knock us off our feet. But I was ready. The smaller mirror in my hand caught the energy and reflected it back toward the larger mirror, the light bending and refracting in a brilliant display of power.

The moment the energy hit the larger mirror, the entire chamber seemed to shudder, the walls trembling as if they might collapse. Franklin screamed in rage and pain, his form flickering and distorting as the energy was turned against him. The surrounding shadows twisted and writhed, as if trying to pull him back into the mirror's depths.

"Keep it steady!" Leo shouted, holding the camera with one hand and bracing himself against the shaking ground with the other. "We're almost there!"

"I won't go!" Franklin screamed, his voice a twisted blend of rage and desperation. "I won't be forgotten!"

"Franklin!" I called out, my voice carrying over the cacophony. "We are going to do your play. We want you to be the star!"

For a moment, just a brief flicker, I thought I saw something in Franklin's eyes—a flash of something human, something broken. In that instant, he weakened enough that a quick thinking Clara and Ethan threw the velvet cover over the mirror.

TYLER REED: TAKE 4

The camera opens with a close-up of Hawthorne Hall's entrance, its heavy doors creaking ominously as they swing open. The scene transitions to the dark, claustrophobic tunnels beneath the theater, where the team cautiously explores with flashlights in hand.

"Welcome back to 'Haunted Histories,' everyone. I'm Tyler Reed, and tonight, we find ourselves deep within the shadowy underbelly of Hawthorne Hall. What started as a search for the truth behind the theater's tragic past has led us to a confrontation with a force more powerful and dangerous than we ever imagined."

The camera cuts to the team gathered in a decrepit dressing room, tension palpable as they stare at a massive, ancient mirror covered with a velvet cloth.

"In our search, we uncovered an artifact—a mirror that seems to pulse with a dark, malevolent energy. This mirror is no ordinary object; it's the anchor that binds the vengeful spirit of Franklin Mason to this theater. For years, his presence has been growing stronger, feeding off the despair and resentment he harbored in life. And now, he's ready to reclaim the spotlight—at any cost."

The scene shifts to the moment the team removes the cloth, revealing the mirror's cracked, shimmering surface.

"But as we uncovered this haunted relic, we realized just how much danger we were in. Franklin's spirit emerged, more tangible and terrifying than ever before, driven by a burning need to be remembered. This isn't just a haunting—it's a battle for control of the very essence of Hawthorne Hall."

"With everything on the line, we made a desperate gamble—to reflect his own energy back at him, using the mirror as both weapon and shield. The result was a showdown unlike anything we've ever experienced, as we faced the full fury of a spirit who refused to be forgotten."

The footage ends with a shot of the team regrouping after the intense encounter, their faces a mix of relief and exhaustion.

"But this battle is far from over. Hawthorne

Hall still holds many secrets, and Franklin Mason's story is only part of the mystery. As we delve deeper into the theater's past, we must prepare for whatever comes next. We must prepare for The Final Act."

CHAPTER 10

The lobby was crowded as people paced back and forth. Several were reading from scripts that had been copied and passed around. Clara was providing instructions to a few others and Tyler was talking to still others.

I was surprised to see Amanda standing off to the side and after catching Ollie's eye; I went to talk to her. Ollie was right behind me. Everyone suspected she had something to do with the fire and while I wasn't convinced, I didn't have any other ideas.

"Amanda, I'm surprised you're here. How did you hear about this?" I asked as we approached her.

She huddled in the corner, her arms crossed over her stomach, watching with large eyes. This was not the take charge woman we had met before.

"Your producer called me. She's supposed to be meeting me here, too. Have you seen her?"

"Rachel? No. Why did she call you?" I was confused. We had just told Rachel the plan a few hours ago, and she was on her way as it was. Why did she call Amanda and was Richard Hargrove going to show up too? Did we really want them here for this very dangerous and challenging thing?

"I don't know why she called me. Well, I have a guess, but-,"

Her words were lost as Rachel rushed up to us.

"Darn, I was hoping to get here first. Glad you made it. Stay right here, okay?" She said to Amanda as she took my arm and steered me away.

"What is going on? Why did you call her?"

"Listen, I found out something very interesting. Franklin Mason is related to Amanda Kerrigan. I wasn't sure if Amanda knew that, but it sure is a coincidence, isn't it? Anyway, when I called her to ask, she admitted it right away. Said she was sort of working undercover and didn't want her boss to know."

Rachel looked around anxiously, as though someone might overhear us. My own mind was racing and trying to make sense of what she was telling me.

"Is she dangerous? Like Franklin?" I asked.

Before she could answer, a few other members

of the team saw Amanda and were standing near her. As I watched, I could tell the conversation was getting heated. Amanda was holding her hands in front of herself and backing away from Leo and Emily. Ollie was standing between them, but as Leo and Emily got closer, Ollie's allegiance was obvious and she turned on Amanda as well.

"What's going on here? Why are they so angry?" Rachel moved through the crowd toward the altercation as I followed her quickly.

"They are upset because she started the fire on stage. It could have harmed us and it caused Leo's computer to be stolen."

That stopped her in her tracks. "What? Amanda didn't start that fire."

"How do you know?" I asked.

"Because I did," she said. "And I took Leo's computer. It's perfectly safe with me, in my car."

"Why the hell would you do something like that?"

I yelled at her as we were working our way through the lobby yet again trying to stop Ollie, Leo, and Emily from doing something harsh.

We reached the small group before she answered me, though, and putting herself between the group and Amanda, Rachel came clean.

"You guys, she didn't do anything. It was me. All me. I wanted to drum up some attention for the show and get the company more invested. Last time you were in danger, Leo, it really helped garner attention. I wanted to do that again, but not get anyone hurt. It didn't hurt anyone, right? Everything was okay."

I couldn't believe she couldn't see how starting a fire like that was innocent or that she couldn't understand why we were angry. And now this person, whom I had zero trust in, had also brought along a relative of Franklin Mason.

"I just can't right now. You two stay right here. We're in the middle of something and we don't need you screwing it up. Come on, guys. We've got work to do," I said.

"I thought the ghost was going to be the scariest part of tonight," Ollie said as we walked away from Amanda and Rachel.

"Yeah, me too. I'm so angry, Ollie."

"I know, me too. Look, we've got this under control out here. Why don't you take a few minutes? Call the studio and let them know what Rachel did. And maybe it will help you calm down."

I knew that would not work at all, but I appreciated Ollie giving me a few minutes to process all that had been going on. With one more look behind me, I darted through the lobby doors and found myself alone in the theater with Franklin's mirror still standing in the middle of the stage under the velvet covering.

I sat in a red velvet seat and leaned my head back. I closed my eyes.

"Hey there, kiddo," a voice to my right spoke.

"Sorry to bother you, hun," a voice to my left said.

Slowly, I opened my eyes to see none other than Ned and Nellie sitting on either side of me.

"We've been watching you and, well, we know all about you."

"Yeah, kid, we know you got the psychic powers and all that. And we know you can handle old Franklin up there easy peasy."

"But we have some thoughts. You know, if you're interested," Nellie added.

I laughed to myself. Of course, this was happening. Again, when it was just me, alone and no way to document. I didn't even have Gabby as a witness. She was hanging out on Clara's shoulder now, whispering ideas into her ear as though they were old pals. The traitor.

Unsure if we were truly alone or if anyone who walked in could see the two of them, I lowered my voice and said, "I would love to hear your thoughts."

As the two vaudeville actors spoke, I listened intently and remembered every single thing they said.

But the most important thing was, Franklin did not start the fire that killed them all.

"Thank you everyone for coming," I shouted. As the crowd quieted and drifted closer to me, I stepped down from the chair I'd been standing on and called Gabby back to my shoulder.

As she landed, she whispered, "You've got this."

"I know all of you are here and prepared to perform Franklin Mason's play, 'The Final Act.' What you may not know is that this theater is haunted. Not just by Ned and Nellie, but also by Franklin. We are here to put Franklin's spirit to rest. I have to be honest, the last time we encountered his spirit, he was angry. And I have nothing to offer any of you except this. I have a feeling. I have a sense that everything will be okay. That Franklin knows what we are doing for him and we will all be safe."

Most of the group looked at me as though I'd just sprouted a second head and I didn't blame them. The younger ones in the crowd literally shrugged their shoulders and went back to practicing their lines as though this were just a fun night out. A few of the older ones in the group looked concerned. Laura Bennett made a beeline for me.

"Are you sure we're safe?" She asked. "We've all heard the stories of how Franklin started the fire that killed Ned and Nellie. Out of jealousy and for revenge. If he's really here, why would he be any different today?"

Just before I could explain that Franklin didn't start the fire, and it was truly faulty wiring, another voice spoke up.

"Because his granddaughter is here," Amanda said. "The story you've heard about him is not the same story I grew up hearing in my family. According to my mother, her father worked so hard to make it big. He wanted to be a star for her. He wanted fame and fortune for his family. Did he want it for himself, too? Of course. He wrote a play, The Final Act, and he sold it for a lot of money. They were going to perform it the night of the fire. It would have changed everything. After he disappeared, my mom grew up without a father. She always said if we could find that play, everything would be different." She turned to me. "That is why I've been so interested. Not because of Mr. Hargrove. Although if he had actually tried to destroy the building, I would have stopped him somehow. This place is just as much my destiny as anyone else's."

Then she looked at the rest of the group. "And I did not start that fire."

This was my chance. "And neither did Franklin," I added. "The first fire started from faulty wiring. That's why all three were killed. They were actually together when the fire started. Franklin was showing Ned and Nellie his script and they were discussing how to perform it. They were all trapped down there at the same time."

"How do you know this?" Ollie asked.

"Ned and Nellie told me," I said simply.

As the small group stood with wide eyes and open mouths, I clapped my hands and made my announcement.

"Tonight, Franklin Mason will be the star of his play. We will begin the action and when it is his turn, we'll uncover the mirror and he will deliver his lines."

A few people snickered but most just nodded as though that were the most normal thing they've ever heard.

"Ollie, Leo, I cannot stress enough how important it is that you both get solid, clear, accurate footage of this."

"No pressure," Ollie said. Then she added, "We won't let you down."

"I'll do my best to help," Clara added. "I think we'll have to invite him in, make it clear that this is his moment, and then guide him through the performance. Franklin's spirit is strong, but he's also been trapped in this loop of longing and regret for so long. If we show him he can finally finish his play, he'll take the opportunity."

Leo, who had been adjusting the cameras, nodded thoughtfully. "So, we set the stage, get everything ready, and then... what? Ask Franklin to take the lead?"

"Pretty much," I confirmed. "We'll start the performance, but we'll leave space for him to step in. We have to clarify that this is his show, his final act. If we do it right, he'll take over."

Jake had agreed to play Franklin's role, and he stepped forward. "And what do I do? Just hand over the role to him when he shows up?"

"Exactly. You start the scene, and when Franklin appears, you step back and let him take it from there. Just follow his lead. If he hesitates, support him—make it clear that he's the star. Are you comfortable doing that?," I asked.

"Yes, of course," he said as Anya and Margaret moved to stand next to him.

"We're all ready," Anya said.

The other actors nodded, their expressions a mix of nervousness and excitement. This was unlike anything they had ever done before, but they were committed to helping save Hawthorne Hall, even if it meant sharing the stage with a ghost.

CHAPTER 11

The team and the actors moved quickly to prepare the stage. The old theater creaked and groaned as they worked, the sense of anticipation building with each passing minute. Leo and Ollie positioned cameras and microphones strategically to capture the performance, while Ethan and Emily made sure the script was ready and accessible.

As the clock in the lobby neared midnight, Clara gathered the group in a circle, her voice steady and calm. "Remember, we're here to help Franklin find peace. He's been waiting for this moment for a long time. If we show him he can finish his play, that he can be remembered, he'll finally be able to move on."

"Alright, everyone. Take your positions," I said.

"Lights, camera, action," Gabby helpfully added.

The actors took their places on stage, the dim lighting casting long, eerie shadows across the worn velvet curtains. We stood just offstage, ready to assist if needed, but fully aware that we were about to witness something extraordinary.

As the clock struck midnight, the air in the theater grew heavy, the temperature dropping noticeably. It was as if the theater itself was holding its breath, waiting for the show to begin.

Jake, standing center stage, took a deep breath and began his monologue, his voice echoing through the empty seats. "To be remembered... is to live forever. To fade into obscurity... is the final death."

As he spoke, the atmosphere in the theater shifted. The lights flickered, and a cold breeze swept through the room. Gabby ruffled her feathers and squawked softly, as if sensing what was about to happen.

And then Clara removed the velvet blanket from the mirror, and a figure materialized. Franklin Mason, dressed in his top hat and coat-tails, slowly stepped forward, his eyes fixed on the audience. He moved with a deliberate grace, as if each step was part of a long-forgotten dance.

The actors froze in place, their eyes wide as they watched Franklin. Jake, true to his word, stepped back and gestured for Franklin to take his place at the center of the stage.

"This is your moment, Mr. Mason," he whispered, his voice carrying through the hushed theater. "Your final act."

Franklin hesitated for a moment, his ghostly form wavering slightly as if uncertain. Then, with a deep breath, he stepped into the spotlight. The room seemed to hold its breath as he began his monologue, his voice strong and clear, filled with the passion and longing that had driven him in life.

"To be remembered is to live forever," Franklin repeated, his voice echoing through the theater. "To fade into obscurity is the final death. But tonight, I shall not fade. Tonight, I take my final bow."

The other actors watched in awe as Franklin moved through the scene, his presence commanding and powerful. It was as if the years of regret and longing had fallen away, leaving behind only the brilliance of a man who had always wanted to be a star.

As Franklin delivered the last lines of the play, the air in the theater grew even colder, the lights dimming slightly. The team and the actors watched in silence, knowing that this was the moment of truth.

"And now," Franklin said, his voice trembling

with emotion, "I leave you with my final performance. A performance that will echo through the ages. Remember me."

With that, Franklin turned to face the empty seats, his ghostly form standing tall and proud. He took a deep, elegant bow, the motion smooth and graceful. As he straightened, the theater erupted in a ghostly applause; the sound reverberating through the hall as if the spirits of Hawthorne Hall were finally giving Franklin the recognition he had always craved.

The applause grew louder, filling the room with a sound that was both eerie and beautiful. Franklin closed his eyes, a look of peace and satisfaction settling over his features. For a moment, he stood there, basking in the applause, his spirit glowing with a soft, ethereal light.

And then, as the applause faded, so did Franklin. His form grew fainter, the surrounding light dimming until he was little more than a shadow. With one final, serene smile, Franklin Mason disappeared, leaving behind only the memory of his last, triumphant performance.

The theater fell silent, the energy in the room shifting from tense anticipation to a calm, peaceful stillness. It was over. Franklin had taken his final bow, and his spirit had finally moved on.

I let out a breath I hadn't realized I was holding. I glanced up and saw Ned and Nellie in the rafters, both wiping tears from their eyes and applauding enthusiastically. Gabby suddenly flapped her wings and let out a cheerful squawk. "Bravo! Bravo!"

The team and the actors exchanged smiles, the tension in the room easing as they realized what they had just accomplished. It was a victory—not just for them, but for everyone who had ever loved Hawthorne Hall.

As the lights in the theater slowly returned to their normal brightness, Ollie turned to me. "We did it. We really did it."

Clara wiped a tear from her eye. "That was... something else. I've never seen anything like it."

Amanda stood with her hands clasped over her heart. Her tear-streaked face turned upward.

Jake, still standing on stage, looked down at the spot where Franklin had stood. "I think we all just witnessed history."

"Yes, we witnessed it, but did we document it?" Ethan asked.

Leo and Ollie raced to the lobby.

After frantically hitting keys and twisting knobs, Leo let out a loud yell while Ollie screamed, "Nooooooo!"

"Jackie, I don't know how we're going to spin this," Rachel said. "I mean, you have some stuff, but is any of it really usable?"

I refrained from punching her in the face as I thought about the video we did actually have that she now had in her car. Then I thought about how she almost got us hurt with her stupid fire scheme. I had very little patience for this kind of questioning.

"I don't know, Rachel. I need a minute, okay?"

After the excitement of the play and successfully sending Franklin to peace, only to find out that every single bit of the video and audio had been damaged, the only people on earth angrier about it than me were Leo and Ollie.

As I stood with my back to the group, they both came up to me.

"Sis, we are so sorry."

"Yeah, Jackie. I just don't know what happened," Leo added.

I sighed. "I know guys. It's okay. We aren't the first and we won't be the last to witness things like this, but not have it documented. The supernatural just doesn't want to be on camera."

"Here, let's go in here where it's quieter and we can talk." Ollie pushed open the theater doors, and we walked into the cool theater. The crowd in the lobby was still celebrating, but as soon as the heavy doors closed, it was quiet again.

We sat in the closest seats, Leo, Ollie and me, and we closed our eyes. The success of the show rested with the three of us, equally at this point. Tyler, Ethan, and Emily had all done their jobs spectacularly. We were the three who messed up.

"Oh, darling, did you see his face?" Nellie's voice rang out across the stage. "He finally got his bow, but it only took him a century or so." She giggled.

We opened our eyes and looked at each other, but no one moved a muscle.

From the side of the stage, Ned appeared, twirling his cane and adjusting his bowler hat with a practiced flourish. "I'd say it was about time, wouldn't you, Nellie? Though I have to admit, the old boy did put on quite a show."

Nellie materialized next to Ned, her ghostly form glowing with a warm, gentle light. She looked every bit the vaudeville star she had once been, her sequined dress shimmering as if it were brand new. "Oh, absolutely, Ned. He had the audience eating out of his hand, didn't he?"

Ollie and Leo sucked in their breath, but none of us dared say a word.

"What will become of us now?" Nellie asked with a pout. "You don't want to leave, do you?"

"No, do you?" Ned asked.

Nellie shook her head, her ghostly bob bouncing. "Not one bit, love. We've been part of this theater for so long. It's our home. And besides, I've grown rather fond of this town and its people."

Ned nodded. "I'm not eager to shuffle off this mortal coil, if you know what I mean."

"But do you think we'll have a choice? I mean, now that Franklin's moved on, doesn't that mean we're supposed to as well?"

"It just might be that's our choice, my dear," Ned said.

"Oh, that would be lovely," Nellie exclaimed.

Out of nowhere, music played, and the couple danced slowly around the stage.

"Watch me, Ned!" Nellie squealed. "In heels and backwards!"

"You are a star!"

When the song finished, the couple stood together, arms around the other, lost in each other's eyes.

"Oh, Neddie, I do wish we didn't have to destroy their machines. They seemed so sad."

"I know, darling. But it's just the way, isn't it? We can't perform for a full house every single night and if everyone knows about us, we would never get to rest."

"I know you're right, of course. But I do wish we could give them just one little thing."

"Come with me, darling. I have an idea." Ned waggled his eyebrows.

And with that, they disappeared from before our eyes.

"I am literally speechless," Ollie said.

"Yeah, I mean...wow," Leo added.

"Well, I guess we know what happened to the documentation," I added. "It wasn't anyone's fault."

"I still feel guilty," Leo added.

"I know. I do too. But we can't fight something like this," I said. "The company will just have to accept it. We've got some footage from before, and we have what Rachel so kindly stole from us. That's enough. Remember, this is more about telling the stories than it is about proving ghosts exist. Yeah, of course, the evidence would be amazing, but we still have a great show."

I stood up and held out my hands. "Come on, let's celebrate with everyone else. This was a good night!"

"Yeah, we need to get a photo of everyone too," Ollie added.

The festivities were ending, but before anyone left, Ollie directed everyone back to the stage while Leo arranged them. As always, Gabby perched on my shoulder, squawking out directions like she was the director herself.

When Leo had the automatic camera set up on the tripod, he joined the group. "Say cheese!" Gabby squawked.

The flash illuminated the grand, decaying stage one last time before we followed the crowd back to the lobby.

"Let's pack up and spend the night in a hotel," I suggested. No one argued with me.

TYLER REED: TAKE 5

The camera opens with a view of the worn, faded stage of Hawthorne Hall, now bustling with people preparing for an extraordinary event. The atmosphere is charged with anticipation as the team makes their final preparations for the night's performance.

"Good evening, everyone. I'm Tyler Reed, and welcome back to 'Haunted Histories.' Tonight, we're not just exploring the past—we're rewriting it. Here, in the heart of Hawthorne Hall, we're about to give Franklin Mason, the forgotten actor, the final bow he's waited a century for."

The scene shifts to show the actors gathering on stage, practicing their lines as Gabby perches on Jackie's shoulder, offering a reassuring, "You've got this."

"This isn't just any performance. Tonight, the

cast will bring to life Franklin Mason's unfinished play, 'The Final Act,' in a bid to lay his restless spirit to rest. But there's more at stake than just putting on a show. For Franklin, this is his chance to be remembered—not as a man consumed by jealousy, but as the star he always dreamed of being."

The camera cuts to an interview with Amanda Kerrigan.

"Tell us about your grandfather," Tyler says.

Amanda takes a deep breath and looks at the camera.

"The truth, as it turns out, is more complex than the legends would have us believe. Franklin didn't start the fire that took the lives of Ned and Nellie Harper. Instead, he was trapped alongside them, his dreams of stardom cut short by tragedy. The play he wrote, The Final Act, has been recovered and a broadway producer, I can't say who, has bought the rights. So not only will my grandfather have his moment of stardom, my family name is restored, and the play that has meant so much will be performed for all to see."

The camera cuts back to Tyler.

"While Franklin Mason's spirit found peace, the team did not.

The scene shifts to the next morning, as the team gathers to review the footage. The mood is somber as they discover that all their recordings have been mysteriously damaged.

"In the end, it wasn't about the footage. It was about the story—Franklin's story, Ned and Nellie's story, and the story of a theater that refused to let its history fade into obscurity. And thanks to the team's efforts, we can say Hawthorne Hall's ghosts aren't just legends—they're a part of its legacy."

"This is more than just a ghost story. It's a reminder that the past is never truly gone, and that even in death, we can leave a mark on the world. Hawthorne Hall will stand as a testament to that— both for the living and the dead."

"I'm Tyler Reed. Thank you for joining us for this episode of Haunted Histories. Be sure to tune in next week for our next adventure."

CHAPTER 12

The next day, as we were packing the van and preparing to leave town, Leo came running up to me.

"You won't believe this," he said. "Look."

He handed me the camera and directed me to look at the image. It was the shot he took of the entire group the night before.

"I can't see anything. I need my glasses." I fumbled around for them and found them on my head.

"What am I looking for?" I asked, squinting at the small screen.

"What? What is it?" Ollie came up beside me and peered over my shoulder.

"Oh, my gosh! Will you look at that?"

I still wasn't seeing what they saw and Leo made the screen bigger.

There, standing in the background of our group shot, were the unmistakable figures of Ned and Nellie. They were side by side, smiling warmly, as if they were part of our team, which, of course, they were.

"We have to show Laura," I said as I swiped at a random tear. "Let's stop by the historical society on our way."

When Laura Bennett saw the photo, she was overcome with emotion. "This is exactly what we needed," she said. "The community will rally behind this. We'll frame it and hang it in the theater's lobby. This is what will help save Hawthorne Hall. Amanda, come look at this."

I was surprised to see Amanda Kerrigan, not in her usual smart suit and heels, but now in faded jeans and an old t-shirt. Laura explained that after learning of her own connection to the theater and a few air clearing conversations the night before, they decided to work together to keep the theater open.

"We're renaming it, too," she added. "The Harper Mason Center for the Arts."

"And this photo will be blown up and hung in the lobby for all to see," Amanda added.

"Another terrific job," Roger Pinnacle announced.

This time, it was just Rachel and me sitting in his office.

"I wish you kids would get some clearer footage. You know that would really help sell the show. But as it is, seems folks like your story telling and don't seem to care too much if they see a ghost or not. Did you see a ghost? No, don't tell me, it doesn't matter."

I wanted to ask about our next investigation, but I couldn't seem to get a word in edge-wise.

"Okay, well, great meeting. Nice seeing you Jackie. I'll see you again."

And he swiveled around in his chair, his back to both of us. Rachel looked at me and shrugged as we gathered our belongings and got up to leave.

The door to the office opened and Mr. Pinnacle's assistant, I still didn't get his name, motioned for us to exit.

"Thank you for coming. We'll be in touch," he said, pushing the elevator button for us.

"Right, but what about the next assignment?" Rachel said. "I'm the producer. Shouldn't I be in on this?"

He only smiled and when the elevator doors opened, he directed us inside. He waved as the doors closed.

"This is the craziest place," I muttered.

"Yeah, it really is. Hey, Jackie, while I've got you. I wanted to apologize again for the fire stunt. I promise I never meant to hurt anyone and never would have done that if I'd thought for a minute someone could be hurt. I think I was a little over-enthusiastic about this being my first job. I wanted it to be a hit."

I nodded as she spoke. I definitely understood that feeling. I decided life is too short to hold a grudge, and she had stood up for us on multiple occasions. While I still didn't completely trust her, and would definitely be watching her, I decided to forgive her.

When the elevator doors opened in the lobby, Amanda said, "You go on. I've got something to do. I'll be in touch."

The doors closed again, and I stood there watching the numbers increase. She had gone back up to Mr. Pinnacle's office.

Ethan and Clara were officially a couple now. Emily had asked if they were going to get married and they both laughed.

"At our age? And this would be number three for me and number two for him. No, we're just going to enjoy life and be 'partners.'" She said, putting air quotes around the word.

Ethan pulled me aside nervously. "Jackie, I wanted to tell you, ah..." he hesitated.

I didn't need to be psychic to know what he was going to say. "I know, Ethan. You're resigning. I understand completely. We have Emily, who will get a nice raise and a new title. We will miss you, but you deserve this. Go enjoy life."

"I'm always here for you. In fact, we both are. Clara would be crushed if you didn't call on her again."

As if on cue, my phone buzzed in my pocket. I pulled it out, half-expecting another crisis, but it was just a text from Rachel.

"Can we meet? Bring the team."

"Well, it looks like we might have something for you soon," I said.

I gathered everyone, and we waited for Rachel.

"What's up?" I asked when she arrived.

She grinned, holding up her phone like a prize. "I just got a confirmation from the office. Who likes college football?"

"Oh! Me!" Ollie exclaimed.

"I do!" I added while, at the same time, Emily's hand shot up.

We looked at Leo and Tyler, who both sat staring at us.

"Alright, looks like the women like their sports! No matter, this isn't about the game per se. It seems a university in Tennessee is having some problems under their stadium, and they need us to take a look."

"Under the stadium?" Emily asked, her eyes widening. "You mean, like, in the tunnels?"

"Sort of," Rachel replied, her grin widening. "But it's not really tunnels. Apparently, the area used to be part of the university's forensic anthropology department—an old facility where they studied human remains."

A shiver ran down my spine. "And what exactly is the 'situation' they're dealing with?"

"That's the fun part," Rachel said, her tone shifting into that dramatic voice-over mode Tyler always used. "Rumor has it that ghosts from rival schools have started causing disturbances, especially on game days. The noise, the crowds... they're not too happy about it."

"Ghosts of rival schools?" Leo repeated, raising an eyebrow. "You're telling me we're dealing with some sort of spectral sports rivalry?"

"Seems that way," Rachel replied, shrugging. "Apparently, they've been causing all kinds of problems—equipment malfunctioning, strange noises, even a few injuries."

"Ghosts of football fans?" Ollie mused, a smirk playing on her lips. "Now that's a new one."

"But seriously, how are we supposed to deal with a bunch of angry college spirits?" Emily asked, crossing her arms. "It's not like we can just ask them to quiet down."

"That's exactly why we've been called in,"

Rachel said, her expression growing more serious. "The university wants us to figure out what's going on and, if possible, put an end to it before the next big game. Apparently, things have been getting worse lately. And there's a rumor that one of the spirits was a serial killer in life."

My blood immediately ran cold. It was long assumed Sophie had met her fate at the hands of a killer who had done this before. This one was likely to be very personal.

Ollie looked at me, concern clear on her face.

"Rachel, do you know about..." her voice trailed off as she darted her eyes towards me.

"Yes, I do." Rachel took my hand. "This might be really tough on you, but you are the absolute best for this one. Are you up for it?"

I felt a tiny nudge in the back of my mind. Whoever killed Sophie had never been caught. If this was true, was it possible this is who took her? What were the odds here? Was I overthinking already? Either way, yes, I was absolutely up for it and I told her that.

We agreed to hit the road the next day.

As I packed that evening, a small part of me couldn't shake the feeling that we were heading into something far more complicated than just a few restless spirits. The ghosts of a hundred years might have been laid to rest, but the ghosts of college rivalries? That was a whole different game.

Will Jackie finally come face-to-ghostly-face with her sister's killer? Find out in **Spooked at Smoky Stadium**, book 3 in the *Haunted Histories series!*

I'd love to stay in touch! If you would like to receive free monthly updates, sneak peeks, and specials, join my Patreon!

If you enjoyed this book, please consider leaving a review or star rating. It's one of the best ways to support independent authors and it lets others know if they might also enjoy this book.

ALSO BY LYNN M. STOUT

Scan above to receive sneak peeks, updates, and special deals by joining my free Patreon!

Find more books by Lynn M. Stout and other cozy mystery authors at the independent book store dedicated to cozy mystery readers!

Visit Mystic Valley Press by scanning the code above.